For Mr. Raindrinker

For Mr. Raindrinker

a novel of New Orleans

Ken Fontenot

ALAMO BAY PRESS

SEADRIFT•AUSTIN

Cover Art: Mina Zavala Lanzas
Book Design: ABP

For orders and information:

Alamo Bay Press
Pamela Booton, Director
Lowell Mick White, Editor / Diane Wilson, Activist

825 W 11th Ste 114
Austin, Texas 78701
pam@alamobaypress.com
www.alamobaypress.com
www.alamobaywritersworkshop.com

Fontenot, Ken.
   For mr. raindrinker: a novel / Ken fontenot
   pages cm
   LCCN 2015946426
   ISBN 978-0-9908632-7-4

1. New Orleans (La.)--Fiction.   I. Title.

PS3557.R79B56 2015

813'.54—dc22   QBI15-600070

For Sheila

Mostly I want you to know the inexpressible feeling when you're crying and your best friend tells you a joke, and you're crying and laughing at the same time.

Disclaimer & Acknowledgments

If anyone takes the characters or events in this story as personal, forget it. I dreamed the story. I have a good unconscious and an even better imagination. As for the wonderful real-life people I mention, I hope they know they'll belong to the ages without my well-meaning, but ultimately meager help.

Contents

For Mr. Raindrinker

New Orleans, Late Seventies

Chapter One

1.

Mostly, I'll tell it the way it is, or has been, which means that someday I'll probably have to get the hell out of here and hide out, maybe in the mountains.

The only two people I'm desperately looking for right now are Mary Lamont whom I still love from eight years ago and Steve Smith who owes me a thousand bucks. But I've lost track of both of them, and really I oughta hire a private detective or somethin', but that's more money than I have right now.

I'm standing on the corner of Franklin Avenue and Gentilly Boulevard, waiting for the bus. From nowhere this black dude walks up and says, "Hey man, don't I know you from somewhere?" He looks real familiar, but we both have to think a few minutes. "Grand Chene," he says. "Oh, yeah," I say, taken aback by his sudden aggressiveness.

We both spent several months in Grand Chene. It's a state hospital across Lake Pontchartrain. He was psychotic, and I was psychotically depressed.

"Can you let me have thirty cents?"

"Uh, well," I hesitate a moment. I don't usually

encourage panhandling, but this guy knew me before. I mean, what was I supposed to do? I really don't have the money to give away, even thirty cents, so I demur.

"Say, brother, I really don't have it myself." Before I can look up he's already mingling with some of the others at the bus stop, asking them God knows what, and making friends with complete strangers.

The bus comes, and we get on, still he doesn't sit next to me. He's already gone up to the driver and starts talking to him. After the driver gives him a pen, he brings the crumpled job listing section of his newspaper to me, asking me to write down my name, address, and phone number. At first, I figure I'll just make one up, so he won't come bothering me. Yet I feel obliged somehow to tell the truth. In a strange way there's something about this guy that's likeable. I write: Kent Soileau, 123 West View Drive, 381-0001. (My surname is pronounced "Swallow.") I don't think he'll really come to my house. He'll probably just throw it away.

"Thanks, man," he says.

"You still taking medicine?" I ask.

"Yeah, and you?"

"Me, too, but only because I can't sleep at night."

He looks real spaced out. His mouth looks very dry. I think he just wanders around the city, changing from bus to bus and never really getting off. Poor guy. Maybe they'll have to put him back in the hospital. It's sad, sad.

I really didn't intend to go to the state hospital. It just happened. One day I just started feeling funny inside. I was reading a book on the execution of the Jews during the Second War, and I started feeling kind of dizzy, then I cried a little. I told my girlfriend I wanted to sleep in the swimming pool. (We were living together in an apartment complex.) I told her I felt violent inside and started banging on the walls uncontrollably. She called the coroner's office and had me committed. She was kind of shaken up and confused about the whole thing, you know, when it's the first time it happens to you. I really wanted her to chain me to the bed post till I got over it, but she wouldn't do it.

The only other person I can actually tell my stories to is my brother. He works at a hamburger place. Sleeps most of the day when he's not working. (I put him down a lot when we were younger. Once I took a swing at him for wearing my shirts and using my toothbrush.) Still, he's a good listener, so I tell him a story about Grand Chene. He's dressing now to go to work, and I'll have to make the story short. By the way, since I'm unemployed, I live with my parents. My father is away on a business trip. My mother is in the hospital having a hysterectomy. My brother is standing by the clothes dryer, waiting for his shirt to come out fresh and hot as apple pie.

It's the weekend at Grand Chene; my girlfriend visits me. We sit on wrought iron chairs in the big yard. We talk about driving to lots of places.

A lady walks up to us. She seems puzzled. She speaks in an expressionless monotone. "Have you seen my comb?"

"No, I'm sorry," I say.

"Well, that was a good comb, and I didn't want to lose it."

"Yes, ma'am."

She's all dolled up. You can hear her whispering to this group of guys, "Look but don't touch." She holds a cigarette in her hand as if it were there for hours: middle-aged, slightly heavy for her tiny frame, wears a kerchief. She notices my T-shirt with TULANE PHYSICAL EDUCATION written on it.

"Oh, you went to Tulane? My husband and son both went there. Husband's deceased, you know, only forty-four with heart trouble. I really must give you this cookie recipe. By the way, my name is Lora Phillabaum."

"Thanks, but I really couldn't accept the gift. I think it's hospital rules."

"That's OK. I make friends easily."

So we took the cookie recipe. She's about to tell us about her son, but the attendant yells out "dinner time" just in time to fish us out.

There is no ashtray around, so he flicks the ashes into the cup of his hand and blows the smoke — one ring after another — into perfect circles. I put my finger through the doughnut of smoke, and it disappears. The smoker is Rudy.

He hesitates. "Can't I smoke on this ward?" he asks.

"Well," the ward chairman says, "you're really not supposed to." He is also an attorney, in here for anxiety and alcoholism. He's used to trouble. He isn't going to be bullied.

"Aw, c'mon," Rudy says. He just got in a few days ago.

"You can smoke in the waiting room if you like."

"Nope, I'm gonna smoke right here," Rudy says, running all ten fingers through his hair.

"You're only hurting yourself. Would you like to go back to the D-1 ward and start all over?"

"OK, I'll be good." The gray stubbles of his beard have gone untrimmed for days. "And I want a good nurse, not just any nurse."

"Would you quit playing games," the ward chairman says in a much stronger voice than before. Silence for a while. Rudy's arms tighten, then his face, and pretty soon his whole body.

I've been standing far away from all this, not wanting to get involved. Now things are getting out of hand.

"Harold, get the leather cuffs," the attendant shouts.

It takes two of them to hold Rudy down, and a third to fit the cuffs on his arms and ankles. The ward chairman says: "give him fifteen or twenty minutes and he'll cool off." Right now Rudy is kicking, arms and legs.

The guy in bed sixteen laughs all the time, even to himself. His laughter is like a bad case of hiccups that builds on itself. If he sees me write a letter, he laughs. There is a cumulative effect to all this, since for a joke he laughs twice as hard.

I sit by the window reading Thomas Mann's *Magic Mountain*. I re-read the chapter "Snow" several times. I speak very little, but when I do, my voice attracts the inmates for advice.

"I didn't like you at first," Charlie, the black dude, says, "but since I saw you play basketball last night, I like you." Charlie believes he knows all the heavy-weight fighters east of the Mississippi. He also says he flew to Africa to personally congratulate Mohammad Ali.

"I know them like brothers," he says. "Some of them are my cousins." You could mention any subject to Charlie, and he would claim to be a master at it. It's like people telling you they are descendants of Pocahontas. A school chum of mine told me that in the fifth grade, and just not to feel bad about having no famous relatives or ancestors, I said I was a descendant of Napoleon. But now, to Charlie's megalomania I say I just don't buy that and point my feet in the direction of the door.

Charlie has to grab my arm to keep me. "And do you know," he says, "I can prove that parallel lines meet?" He starts explaining so fast that I can't tactfully pull out.

"Einstein, you see, was really an idiot, and this is how I'll show you." On a piece of brown paper he tears from a grocery sack he draws an imperfect circle, using only his shaky hand. He calls it earth.

"Just as we have nine systems in our bodies, we have nine planets. Understand?"

"I think so."

"Well, if you fit bars of music—you didn't know I played in a band, did you—fit bars of music onto the earth you'll see what I mean." I raise my finger.

"Now please don't interrupt, you white honky. Ha! Ha!"

I am concerned about people who laugh so maliciously. "But I wasn't interrupting," I say.

"Well, OK," he says, and places nine whole notes across the grid, attaches a treble clef to it and says, "there you go."

"That's all?"

"Yep," and he starts telling me about his college career.

I whisper to myself: "Like hell he went to college." I'm puzzled. "But I thought you were going to prove parallel lines eventually intersect."

"I just did. Man, can't you see anything?"

"Sure." Confused and annoyed, I do an about face without saying anything and walk off.

Almost every time a nurse or an attendant unlocks the door from the outside, inmates hear the jingle of the keys from that outer world coming in. They flock to her pill and needle tray like pigeons. And they must be thinking how much it's gonna hurt (if it's a needle), and will the next time give them the inner peace they hope for.

Take, Tony, for example, no real inner peace, in here for heaven knows what else. He says the cops chased him all the way from Westwego to Marrero. He's doing 120 in his 1964 Chevy hot rod. The car is so blue it looks black in the night. That cop could have called for a roadblock, but he wanted Tony for himself. Tony loses him turning the corner in Marrero, the one the State Farm Insurance office is on. Once again he escapes the flypaper that is his police record.

There are only two of us on the ward that faintly resemble Groucho Marx. The other guy looks more like Groucho, but I win the look-alike contest cause my voice resembles Groucho's. His most resembles Ed Sullivan. You ask him to do an impression of John Wayne, James Stewart, Kirk Douglas, and Jimmy Cagney, and they all come out kind of close to Ed Sullivan. I can do all those pretty well. It's a hobby of mine. Before I came here, I would tape all their voices and practice them.

The PR director of the hospital tells us a camera crew of a local TV station is coming out to take pictures of me in my baggy black pants, thin necktie, cigar, black hair parted down the middle, black moustache covering the width of my lip, and thick black brows. (The latter two were done with black grease paint.)

They film me walking down a sidewalk doing a duck walk, wagging my Havana like a tail. "This is the most ridiculous thing I ever heard of," I mimic only six inches in front of the camera lens. Then: "Once I shot an elephant in my pajamas. How he *got* in my pajamas, I *still* haven't figured out." At six o'clock I'm propped up to see the TV. News, sports, weather, but no me. I wait for the 10 o'clock news. The whole ward cheers when they see me. I see myself. It's spooky.

Thursdays are music therapy. We get in a circle and write down how we feel especially about symphonies. The choices are: good, bad, confused, pretty, ugly, happy, sad. The group leader is about to put on a record.

"The farthest I've been from here is Jackson,

Mississippi. We lived —"

"That's nothin'. I've lived in California."

Other states come up as the farthest they've been from here in Grand Chene.

The record plays. It's "Switched on Bach" using the Moog synthesizer. Up to now Mr. Phelps has his head bent down to his chest, fooling around with his Jesus cross. He wears a T-shirt saying CHALMETTE HIGH SCHOOL PHYS ED. He gets more and more jumpy, steps across the room, takes a chair, still looks at the group. He sketches the girl next to me with a crayon that lies next to a coloring book. The rest of us are listening quietly to Bach. Phelps walks up to the girl.

"See if you can guess who this is in the group." Silence.

"I don't really know," the girl says.

"Go ahead, take a guess." More silence. Except for Bach. I'm thinking: there's a time and a place for everything, and this is not the time for art.

Phelps walks over to me to show his wallet with all kinds of cards in it. He back-tracks to his seat, props his hand behind his head, and cracks his knuckles.

Phelps is really annoying me now. We're both drunk on drugs, except his jaw bone moves all the time (mine moves much less). I ask him if this proverb meant anything: the tongue is the enemy of the neck. He says no it didn't.

"It means watch out what you're saying, and who you say it to, or you might lose your neck."

"Hmm. Never would have thought of it that way."

"I notice you have something in your top pocket," I say.

"Yeah, cartoon blocks."

"Really?"

"That's right. I cut them out of comic books and stack them up and flip them one at a time. I follow the story better that way." Pause. "See this coupon from the back page? Also, I'm sending off for the Charles Atlas body-building manual."

He was using the comic book I bought for my sister. He must have stolen it from my room. He's real annoying, so I throw a punch at him, miss, and hit the wall instead.

I tell the doctor later I got it slammed in a car door, since I'm embarrassed about hitting the wall. But the clever doctor shows me the X-ray and says: "See that bone, how it's cracked. Looks like a fighter's break."

"Doc," I say, "I'd like to file a claim with the insurance."

"Oh, I see, I'll just tell them you got it caught in a car door."

"Thanks."

Now I wear a cast for the second time in my life. People ask me how I got the cast, and I've memorized at least ten different stories I made up. My cast is a white tree trunk where everybody signs his or her name.

The whole ward is taking this too seriously. Half want to watch the World Series, and half want to watch a variety show. So they decide that if they can't decide then nobody watches TV, and it stays off.

I go to my bunk, lie down, and count holes in the ceiling.

I meet Charlie the talker one day when his parents come. His father is staring down at his own black and shiny pointed lace-ups. Charlie tells us he's sure he's an astronaut, and his mother's face grows tense. Charlie says to me: I'll have to take you out on my latest discovery, an anti-gravity machine that uses perpetual motion to power it.

Finally, after five months in the place I'm discharged. I drive to the highway — my girlfriend's with me — and onto a parking lot where I'll pick up a prescription. Right in the middle of the lot this lady dumps those cups, straws, and sacks you get from McDonald's. I'm furious. I walk up to her on the driver's side, speaking at her nose to nose. "Why don't you throw your own trash into your own living room?!" She is visibly moved. "Y-, Y-, Y-, You must be insane!" I can't argue with that.

Oh, yes, and did I tell you, my second girlfriend ever, the one who came to visit me at Grand Chene, finally split up with me. We had been living together for two years. One day at 2330 Frenchman Street she starts crying and says she's doing all the responsibilities that I'm supposed to be doing, like washing the dishes, and she wants to go home to her mother in Dallas. So we load up all her furniture in a U-haul truck, and I drive her five hundred miles back to Dallas. Back home now, I get teary-eyed. Call her up asking forgiveness, and can we get back together, but she says it's too late, we had our chance. So what's a guy supposed to do?

I especially remember one scene from our relationship near the end of it. She was combing her hair in the dresser mirror. I was lying across the bed only half settled in.

"I'm playing the bingo game at the supermarket," she says.

"Really?"

"Yes."

"Think you'll win?"

"I don't think so. I'm not lucky when it comes to things like that."

The TV was loud in the other room. She sets her brush down, walks in the living room, and turns it low. She goes back to the mirror.

"Think I'm getting skinny?" she asks.

"I don't know. Let me see." I get up to look, approach her from the rear, and squeeze her breasts. I'd do that too, in the supermarket, when no one was around.

"Sure, you're looking thinner."

"Do you think I can wear my shorts tonight?"

"I guess so." And a few days later, for some reason, I cursed her out: it was all over.

An almost cloudless day into whose blue one's joy ascends. Walking along Decatur Street, I can see the tops of a few ships tied up along the Mississippi River. Only enough money in my pocket to have *café au lait* and beignets among the tourists. Here I first run into Raindrinker as he folds balloons for kids near the Café Du Monde. He's wearing a clown suit and a painted face similar to Clarabel's, which brings to mind the *Howdy Doody Show* of 1950s television, Clarabel's hair coiffed in that funny clown style, unruly and probably flaming red. One kid, plump as a Christmas turkey on the table, asks for a giraffe, and Raindrinker, with all his powers, makes one in an amazingly quick minute or so, without even bursting a balloon. My talent is doing impressions of famous personalities, but this balloon folding is a skill I have long admired. When he does his twisting, you can hear the noise of balloon against balloon, a squeaky sound, as if made by mice.

All those standing around applaud and say "yeah!" the minute Raindrinker hands the kid the giraffe he has just given birth to. His tip jar is loaded with ones and fives. Tips are all he asks for. Raindrinker holds up a sign that says: THAT'S ALL FOLKS FOR NOW. SEE YOU AGAIN SOON. I linger while the crowd disperses. A flock of pigeons flutters up and circles a lap around both Pontalba apartments. Raindrinker's eyes lock onto mine.

"Would you like, say, a doggie balloon (a dachshund maybe) for your son or daughter?"

"No, thanks, I was just standing here admiring your art."

"Thank you. Where ya from?"

"Oh, I'm a local boy."

It turns out we both went to the same high school on St. Claude Avenue near the Industrial Canal. However, he was five years older, Class of 1960.

He tells me everyone called him Mr. Raindrinker, a sort of nickname. He says once as a boy he put a glass under the rain gutter spout during a shower, drank it, and his father said: "That's a good idea. A rain drinker." The name stuck, first with his family, then with all his friends.

I ask him if he has a favorite watering hole.

"Yeah, the Rusty Nail in the Carrollton area."

"I go there a lot, too," I say, "Good live music on the weekends, women to dance with, and booze at reasonable prices."

"Maybe I'll run into you down there," he says, packing his equipment.

"Yeah, I like to ride the streetcar out that way, even some weekday evenings."

I shake his hand. Walk around Jackson Square to observe tourists getting their portraits done. Ah, yes, I guess you could say I'm a people watcher at heart.

I'm alone now, and here are some of my feelings in my room late at night:

The cola still goes down my throat and burns. My socks still smell, and each morning the trees still burn in the east. Lately, anything I aim at the wastebasket I miss. Looking over these words I find I've forgotten to take off my jacket.

Sometimes, nights like these, past midnight, when I can't sleep with excitement, I feel like calling all my friends, long distance.

I wish I knew more about chickens—the only ones I see in the store have no feathers.

All I have on my desk are notes: do this, do that. Tomorrow will not be enough.

My clock has stopped at five twenty.

Right now I'm looking at a picture of me at twelve. I am in a Confirmation robe. I'm not smiling. It must be the dead I'm remembering.

I worked for the government once, for a week or two, and did you know that more air traffic controllers are getting nervous over their jobs, and that our mailmen's most reported injuries have to do with being bitten by dogs?

I'm working a cross-word puzzle. I need a four-letter word for slave. Hmmm.

I have to cheat and look in the cross-word puzzle dictionary. Esne. What a funny word. Esne.

I can sketch a good nose, or a good ear, or a fine pair of eyes, but the trouble comes when I have to sketch the whole face.

The TV crackles when you turn it off. There was no one looking at it before I turned it off, not my brother, not my sister, no one. It's such a waste to leave something on without using it. The same goes for lights.

My brother's girlfriend Nora, who's married and with a child, wants him to take another girl out just to prove his love for her isn't only loneliness. My brother doesn't think it will prove anything, so he is taking this girl Phyllis out reluctantly. They will go to the Beef Baron for supper, and then he'll take her to the top of a revolving restaurant for a drink or two. But even now he tells me: I don't really want to do this, you know, I'm still in love with Nora. They all work for McDonald's hamburger place, and Phyllis, my brother says, is no beauty.

It wasn't only a hysterectomy my mother needed. She also had hydrocephalus. After two weeks in the hospital she came home. At night, at bedtime, my mother would say: Where am I? We'd say: you're home, go to sleep.

Mother: No, I'm not, I'm in a car driving fast, and the next door neighbor's kids are beating up on my kids. Back to the hospital for Mother. This time the mental ward.

Since graduation from college I've worked as a meat cutter, a Pinkerton, an encyclopedia salesman (two days), vacuum cleaner salesman (a week), photographer's assistant (a month), a bookstore stock clerk (I forget how long), a clerk at the State Hospital records center, a staff reporter for a neighborhood newspaper, an employment counselor, a kindergarten teacher (only a week there — the kids generally ran over me, me being Mr. Nice Guy, saying "yes I will" every time one wanted a shoe tied), a clerk at a Federal Government Department of Labor Workman Compensation branch, an assistant manager for a financial loan company. (One week there, having to spend mostly all day threatening people to pay back their loans.) I just recently got a job as a driver for the River Boat Pilot's Association. I drive river pilots to and from the ships they take up and down the Mississippi River.

There is an art in going from job to job, but I'm not sure I can fully explain it. My parents say: sad, sad. My friends say either "that's great" or "when will you find something you like?" I don't know how I feel about it.

That's the truth.

2.

It's late December in New Orleans. The papers say it's one of the coldest winters on record. There was a story in the paper about a girl from Iowa who nearly froze in weather below zero, and who finally, after being turned down by three local farm houses (they never even opened the door, just spoke to her through the door), was picked up by a Greyhound bus and taken to a hospital where she was treated for frost bite.

I've been working for a week now at River Parish

Ship Service on the Mississippi River. (I still live with my parents.) I work from 6pm to 6am, six days on and three days off. It's my first day off. I sleep in the daytime as usual. But on my second day off I try to sleep at night and sleep only fitfully. I have this little dream. My parents, who are both away, have left their separate bedrooms to two beautiful girls, one black and one white. Outside the bedrooms two knights in armor with axes stand guarding the doors. I would risk my life trying to enter both rooms, but Morpheus has me bound and gagged in my own bed. No matter how hard I try, I can't seem to awaken to fight off the guards to the entrance of the rooms of sweet delight....

In the morning a friend of mine from graduate school in Baton Rouge several years earlier calls me. She's living in Austin, Texas now where she took a Masters in German. Her name is Pam Weiss. She's selling her leather crafted wares at an open market near the University of Texas.

"Hi, Pam, I'm glad you thought of me when you were in town."

"Oh, it's nothing. Besides, you called me long distance several months ago. I felt it was the least I could do to get back in touch with you."

It's Saturday night. I suggest we go to the movies, and she agrees. Although New Orleans offers all kinds of places to go to listen to music: jazz, pop, and progressive country, Pam and I were used to doing movies together. Even in college we always went to see a free flick on campus, which the university sponsored. My car is old and in need of repairs, yet I suggest we take it, even though she has a better car. At the movie she insists on paying her own way in and, too, treats me to a Coke and a box of popcorn. The movie is in French with sub-titles. It's about a family in which distant cousins are having affairs with each other: very funny and very French. On the way back to her house we talk of our lives. I have always felt good talking to Pam. True, we have our separate worlds, but I can still discuss personal matters with her and be at ease. Likewise for her.

In fact, we share the honesty of siblings without the disputes that often plague such relationships.

"I guess I told you my girlfriend and I broke up."

"Uh huh, you called me long distance."

"Right. Well, it was a case of her not feeling that I was giving her enough stability, among other things. You know how I was jumping around from job to job, so in the end we decided it was best if I try to make it on my own. I regret the decision now. I call her, hoping to get back together, but she says we had our chance." Feeling I've talked enough, I ask her about her family.

"Oh, my sister ran away from home recently. But the police finally found her in Orlando, Florida. They stopped her because the tail lights in her car were out, and, checking her license, they ran her name through their computer, finding out she was a run-away. She's back in New Orleans now. My mom let her have her own apartment and is sending her to college. She's 17 now. Graduated from high school a year early."

There was a silence for a few minutes. Outside I notice some guy has run a red light. "But let's talk about Amanda for a while."

"I just happen to have one of her last letters here in my top pocket. Care to read it?"

"Sure."

```
Sunday, Dec. 19


Dear Kent,


My how fast this month has gone by. I
hope the winter goes by as fast; we're
having snow again today, and I'm not
```

sure I'll be able to get to work again
tomorrow.

Yes, I do have a steady boyfriend now.
I met him at the Cutlery Place this
Christmas season. He was here when you
called today and doesn't understand
why we can still be friends. You know,
Kent, I could not get back with you—
I've said this before. But I've always
felt you to be a brother to me, and I
care what happens to you. Your strength
is your ability to write. You write
well, and I admire that. When you had
your friends, Susan, etc., you were
free to correspond with them, or call
them if you felt like it. I never felt
resentment or jealousy of your friends,
as you well know. Although we were
unable to work out our relationship,
I nevertheless value your friendship
and communication. I've explained
this to Ed. He's not had many special
friendships like we have. It will have
to be something he needs to accept.

In short, if this kind of arrangement
is acceptable to you, I'll be glad. We
can share our lives with each other.
You can share your poetry (and someday
novel) with me, and we can learn and
grow from that point. You have a lot
of possibility, Kent, but you've got
some growing to do, as I do. The man
I have met is a good man. He's strong
and kind. But what we had together will
never be forgotten. I want to see you

find the happiness you need.

      Life moves forward—it's good for you
      to contemplate past experiences, but
      not to dwell on them. I'm moving on,
      looking for the peace of mind I need,
      and I think we can give each other
      support because we know each other so
      well. I would be interested in your
      views. I also hope you'll send me a
      couple or three of your best poems.
      If you really work, someday you could
      become a good writer. Take care. Please
      say hello to your family for me.

      Amanda

"And can you accept this letter?" she asks.

"Not really. I have a hard time accepting that she's making love to someone else but me."

"Ah, then it's probably not love you still feel for her, but a crushed ego."

"This was not her final answer. I called her last weekend, and she said I'm trying to get back together with her, and she doesn't want this. So she says if I ever call or write, she'll either hang up the phone, or send my letter back to me. That was really crushing."

"I'll bet it was. But look, it's been five or six months since you last saw her, and there really are a lot of other women out there that would be interested in you."

"Yes, but where?"

"Oh, come on, you're not giving up already?"

"No." We pulled up in front of her house. I gave her a big hug and a kiss on the cheeks. She was very receptive. Then she walked away, and I watched her as she unlocked the front door.

Chapter Two

⚜

1.

It's 5 AM. I pick up Captain Miller from his ship, the Australian Bridge. We catch Airline Highway from the River Road and stop at a restaurant in La Place. On top there is a big neon sign with a coffee pot pouring out a cup of coffee. Inside a dozen waitresses are waiting for the morning rush. They gather and touch. They sing along to the juke box. Two guys and two girls walk in and sit down. The girls take their purses and go to the bathroom together. Why do they do that? To hold hands in there? To gossip? Captain Miller and I order grits, biscuits, and scrambled eggs. A young girl walks in, and we ask each other how old we think she is. He says 20. I say 17. She is wearing strong perfume and the sweetness of a face.

Tuesday or Wednesday, one. I could talk about time, but it's been talked about before by Thomas Mann in *The Magic Mountain*. Fact is, I don't remember one day from the rest unless I think. You see, if I come to work on Tuesday night, I get off Wednesday morning. In which case I'd have to remember two dates. And I don't wear a watch. But I'm tired, so I know it's probably Wednesday morning before dawn. I could ask the dispatcher what time it is, yet he's too far away for my radio to reach. My neck aches, and my fingers have a cramp from holding the steering wheel in one spot.

Miles from somewhere, maybe La Place, maybe Sorrento, we're on the Interstate, Captain Miller and I. I am driving him to a ship he will take up to Baton Rouge. I tell him about myself, my family, how I got here, and how I even managed to get a college degree—the first ever in my family. (My grandparents on both sides were sharecroppers in Evangeline Parish.)

"Then will you tell me what a man with a degree and some graduate school is doing driving me around like a cabby?" I am thinking for an answer.

"How much do you make a month, son?"

"600 dollars."

"Do you know what we make? Four thousand dollars a month, and some of these pilots don't even have a third grade education. You should see them at the dinner table. Hogs. I tell you, hogs. They grunt and groan while they eat."

"All of them?"

He didn't answer, started to wipe off the fog on the windshield with the back of his hand so we both could see better.

"What did you study anyway?"

"German literature."

"And you mean you can't find anything that will pay you more? Seems like you've got a lot of brain power going to waste. I think you've sold yourself short. You've got to make a living, you know, and 600 dollars a month is peanuts if you want to raise a family."

"But I like driving pretty much."

"What about becoming a translator or an interpreter?"

"Those jobs are hard to come by, and you have to be really good."

"Well then, I don't want to sound like I'm preaching, but I still think there's something out there more challenging than driving pilots around."

"Maybe you're right. I'll consider it."

"And how old are you now?"

"Twenty-nine."

"Over the hill, wouldn't you say?"

"Oh no, I've just begun to realize it's not how old you are or what you do, but how well you do your job that counts."

"That sounds like something your father might say. Still, if you believe it, it's OK. I really think, though, that a man of your qualifications should be earning more money."

We hear this whining noise like the high-pitched scream of an animal, and then, thud, thud, thud. I pull the car over.

"What was that?" he asks. "Did we hit something?"

"No, just a flat rear tire." He says *shit*.

I get out of the car, walk to the back, and open the trunk. It's so dark I have to grope around for the lug wrench and jack, having no flashlight. I swear to myself that next time I'll bring a flashlight. The momentary lights of passing cars help a little. It's late, however, and there are not that many cars on the road.

I take the lug wrench out first and feel my way over to the injured tire. I jack up the car a bit. I feel the lug nuts with my hand, trying to loosen them with the wrench. It's no use. They're on too tight.

Cap'n Miller gets out of the car and walks to the back. The cold air is already cutting deep, and both of us stand bundled into ourselves.

"No luck here, sir."

"What's the matter?"

"Some bastard put the lug nuts on tight, with an air wrench, probably. I can't get them off."

"Here, let me try." He strains but does no better than I did.

We're lucky that a car stops for us, luckier still that this man has a CB radio in it that can call for help. Although we have a radio in our car, we don't have the frequency of anyone out here in our vicinity. The man in the car tries several stations. At last he finds a man driving nearby, whose son worked in a gas station. "Roger, I'm headed your way, and my son's with me," I hear the radio say. Cap'n Miller is in a hurry. He asks the man if he will give him a lift to Sorrento, where he will take a taxi to his ship.

I wait alone for ten or fifteen minutes. Then a car pulls alongside. It is one of these souped-up things, with the back end higher off the ground than the front, and wide wheels. The man on the passenger side stays in the car. Then a huge man, maybe 300 pounds, gets out. He holds a lug wrench in the shape of a cross, walks over to me, and asks what the problem is.

"Can't get these lug nuts off. Two of us done tried it."

He says nothing. Goes right to work. As he twists and turns his wrench I can feel his muscles tighten.

"Here," he says, "while I pick up on this end, you kick that end with your foot." I do what he says, and within minutes all the lug nuts are loosened.

"Can you take it from here?"

"Sure. How much do I owe you?"

"Oh, about a dollar for a coupla beers."

"Great." I got off real cheap on this one. If a tow truck would have come out, it would have cost at least twenty-five.

I finish changing the tire. Drive back sixty miles to River Parish Ship Service to tell them what happened.

2.

I made three dollars in tips from pilots early this morning: enough to buy breakfast. I hardly ever eat at home. I eat out most often. My parents really don't keep that much food around the house.

I ran several stop lights. What the hell. 4 AM on a Sunday morning. No cops around. I was late to pick up a pilot, so I was speeding along the Interstate when this highway patrolman pulls up alongside. I slow down immediately. But there he is, riding alongside me for about two minutes, staring at my car. I guess he would have given me a ticket if he hadn't read the sign on my door: MARINE TRANSPORTATION, INC. So he must have figured I was on official business, not just some jerk joy-riding and speeding for the hell of it. It was mighty nice of him to drive on without stopping me. I could have just said "it was mighty white of him...." but that's a prejudiced joke against black people, and I really don't like it, though some people think it's cute.

I pick up Captain Peck from an Indian ship. Even as he gets in the car I can smell whiskey on his breath. Then he tells me sort of matter-of-factly that the Captain aboard ship asked him to have first one, then two drinks with him while the crew was busy letting down the gangway. I say good morning. Cap'n Peck immediately starts in.

"You take these Hindus. Real nice people, but very weak. They have to carry a double crew they're so weak at getting the ship tied up. Also they're not practical people. You can give them anything to study from a book, and they'll learn it. I mean really learn it. But as far as common sense goes, no common sense. They do keep a clean ship though. Not like those dirty Greek ships. And you never see the Hindus drunk on shore. The Americans and the Norwegians. Can't hold their booze."

"Oh, really?" I ask.

"Yeah, you saw that drunk American seaman the other night at River Parish Ship Service. He fell on the way down to the launch boat and bloodied his head somethin' awful. Then he stumbles around, so someone can catch him if he falls. And then he pulls out a wad of money stacked with hundred dollar bills. The dispatcher tells him to put his money back in his pocket. No cause for all that foolishness. No cause at all. Americans and Norwegians. Now you take the Japanese, the Koreans, and the Chinese. Clean people. Clean ships. And you never see them come back to their ships drunk. And the chief mates and captain are always dressed in business suits. But not the Americans or the Norwegians. No, sir."

I kind of liked Cap'n Peck best of all the many pilots. Talked a lot, but never bored me. Most of the time when we'd pass through those small towns along the river he'd say, let's stop here and get somethin' to eat and drink. We liked crawfish and beer, and although the crawfish season began in February, some people now raised them year round on special crawfish farms. I'd pull out my money to pay, but he'd insist: "Save your money, it's on me."

Once I ran out of gas on my way to pick him up from

the dock at Burnside, and I was two hours late. When I pulled up he said: damn, what happened? I explained and he said, "oh, I see, well let's get home as fast as we can." Well, most of the pilots would have chewed my ass for an hour.

3.

So this is Star Fleet. The West bank of the Mississippi. Just the end of a road, behind an unlit hospital, leading to the levee, that long, winding hill where you can't go no more except into the river, unless of course you had your seven league boots on, and you could hop it. The river is so wide here that no one can throw a coin across to the other side. It might, just might make it a quarter of the way across.

I'm all alone in car Five, an old Dodge that's seen better days. It is late, one or two AM. All of my work is behind me. Up till now I had to take three pilots home here on the west side after they got off their ships. This is where they make pilot changes. A small crew boat from River Parish across the river will pull along side the big ship while it's still moving, and a new pilot will climb up a rope ladder to change places with the pilot he relieves and take the ship to the mouth of the river. There the ship's Captain will finally take it out to sea.

So I'm alone in the darkness. A few stars out. My radio is on. I can hear the dispatcher giving instructions to other drivers. But for me there's nothing. Up on the levee I watch a man in a sweat suit jogging toward morning. Two hours later the paper boy comes down River Road, his bicycle basket full of today's news. I listen to the radio, the pop tunes bringing back memories of the girl I lost first to friendship then to nothing.

It is cold. I start the engine, press on the heater. After a while it gets too hot, and I kill the engine, and the whole cycle goes on all night. For the hell of it I try my flashlight, but the batteries must be weak. Who could I find in this darkness with this awful flashlight?

Like a child crying, the belly knows if you've cheated it of its due. All night long it can bally hoo, bally hoo, and talk back to you. The belly knows a thing or two, and mine tells me. I start the car and drive to an all night food store where I pick up some milk and a package of cup cakes. I drive back to the base, Star Fleet, turn on the inside light, and read a book of poems. It's pretty bad, so then I thumb through a girlie magazine the daytime driver left under the seat. Soon my night is over. The dispatcher asks me if I want a little overtime, but I say no, I'm pretty tired after twelve hours. He sends the crew boat, the Molly, across the river to pick me up. River Parish is busy with crew boats coming and going every hour, taking sailors to and from their ships anchored in the river.

The dispatcher's cabin is a long walk up the gangway from where the small boats tie up. I walk in. The place is full of sailors talking and telling jokes. One sailor is lying down, his mouth bloodied. Another is being helped to an ambulance, his face green-yellow. I look at his friend questioningly. "Yellow jaundice," he says and turns away.

I usually stay awhile to joke around with the morning drivers, but I'm out of sorts and decide to go home. Sam Marino is reading the racing form. He ruins all the seats in the cars cause he weighs so much. Some guys are playing cards for money: Knock Rummy. I myself never bothered to learn. The dispatcher is busy talking to a pilot on the radio. He recognizes me. "Hi ya doin', sweetheart? You and Al still sweet on each other?" Al was a guy quit a while back. He and I both had college degrees and talked a lot to each other about any kind of art. It's been a standing joke that Al and I were lovers, and the dispatcher teases me a lot. You know, I go along with him. Then he gets up, pinches me on the ass, and says "you sure are cute," trying to make me angry, but it doesn't bother me. "I sure get tired of trying to talk to intellectual midgets," I tell the dispatcher, and that shuts him up pretty quick. I start to walk out, laughing. Him: "OK, cutie, be a smart guy, but let me know when you two get married."

4.

When I graduated from high school eleven years ago, they picked me as most likely to succeed. For a long time I took it seriously and felt bad if I didn't feel like I was a success. But now I don't consider myself either a success or a failure. All I know is I'd like to feel what it's all about to be an old man someday. Maybe that's success enough.

I've learned in the last eleven years how to get out of mostly anything I didn't want to do. This next week, for example, I want to take two extra days off in addition to my regular three so I can take a small vacation and travel. Where I work, though, they don't believe in vacations (at least they don't pay you to go on vacations). So I will have to pretend illness or somethin'. I think I'll say I had to go to the hospital for tests because my doctor thinks I might have polycythemia. Too many red blood cells, you know. I believe it'll work.

Sometimes they can be real bastards at work. Like one day I called in sick, coughing like a maniac, and the dispatcher says: well try to make it in if you can. Come on in. We need you bad. Sickness is for them hardly an excuse. But this thing about my going to the hospital to have tests run will be easier for them to accept than just an ordinary illness like a cold, or diarrhea, or whatever.

They give me the extra days off I ask for, without pay of course. But a week later I'm going to pick up a pilot living off Franklin Avenue, and I fail to yield while making a left turn. A police car hits me broadside. Does a lot of damage. No one hurt, all of us shaken up, our voices quivering while we talk. The police tell me it's my fault. I'm speechless. I tell myself: sure I should have seen them coming, but they were going awfully fast not to have on either their siren or their flashing lights.

It was the third accident I'd had in three months. Everyone at work liked me, but the boss said he had to fire me (no hard feelings, he said). So he did. I've always quit jobs before. It was the first time I'd ever been fired. Inside me I felt those electrical sparks jumping, the kind you see when you ride the bumping cars at an amusement park.

5.

Saturday morning, the morning of my sister's birthday, the phone rings. It's Captain Peck.

"Say fella, I heard you got fired."

"Yeah, but I'm not too worried. I have a friend says he can get me a job offshore on the oil rigs as a cook's helper."

"Great. I just got hold of fifty pounds of boiled crawfish. Can you make it over for about noon and help me eat these things?"

"Sure. Beth, my sister, has a birthday today, and we'll cut the cake about noon, so how bout one?"

"That's fine. Still remember how to get here?"

"Of course, Cap'n. That was part of my job. Getting you home."

"Oh, right. Just wanted to make sure. See you at one."

My sister had been practicing ballet all morning all over the house. It was pretty irritating to me, but my parents didn't seem to mind. She had taken dancing lessons since she was four. One time I asked her if she wanted to be a professional dancer. She told me no, she wanted to be an airline stewardess. Which I found kind of strange. My mother came in the kitchen from sleeping all morning. She weighed about ninety pounds. Before she went to the hospital she weighed in at 140. After she had the hysterectomy, she developed hepatitis. We think she got it from a blood transfusion given to her in the sixties when her lack of energy was diagnosed as anemia. In three months she lost all that weight.

My brother was working, so I went out and bought a cake at the bakery with HAPPY BIRTHDAY BETH on it. There were twenty candles. She blew, missed one, and blew the last one out. I'll bet she wished to meet a rich, handsome guy on some airplane trip to the Bahamas. Who knows?

My father fed the cake to my mother, she still being weak and all. I wanted to tell him to let her feed herself, cause after a while she'd become dependent and revert to childhood. As it was, when she slept, she assumed the posture of a fetus. She could have fed herself if she weren't so stubborn. Any other man but my father would have thrown her out a long time ago for not trying to do things on her own. But I kept silent. I didn't cut myself too big a piece since I'd be eating crawfish soon. As usual, I spilled cake on my good pants. Took a dishrag and rubbed the cake out.

I got to Cap'n Peck's house exactly at one. I was never late to any place. In fact, usually early. My job had taught me punctuality. It was a gorgeous brick home near Lake Pontchartrain, where the wealthy lived. Out front near an old oak was a set of wrought iron chairs. The sidewalk wound snake-like to the front door. I rang the bell. It was no ordinary buzzer. It chimed three or four times.

Cap'n Peck opened the door, looking in good spirits, as always. I've never seen this man sad. He led me through a plush living room to a small, but adequate kitchen. Piles of deep-red crawfish lay on the table, their feelers looking like small TV antennas.

"Get yourself a beer, Kent, and let's get started."

I opened the refrigerator. It was full of only beer and more crawfish wrapped in newspaper. The only other things were a jar of mayonnaise and half an onion, drying out. I imagined he and his wife ate out a lot. Just for curiosity's sake I checked the freezer. As I expected, only a half-eaten box of ice cream.

I opened my beer, sat down, and dug in. On each crawfish I pulled head from tail, peeled off the shell around the tail, ate it, and sucked the head for the yellow fat that was really tasty. Not everybody did this, but I was a real Cajun. (At least my parents were.)

I noticed his wife wasn't eating with us, but I didn't ask why. We had pretty much cleaned up the pile we started on, leaving the heads and pieces of shell in another great pile on the other side of the table. The Cap'n wiped his hands with a wet cloth and passed it to me.

"Kent, there's a favor I have to ask of you."

"What's that, sir?" There was a long pause.

"I don't know exactly how to say this, but my wife and I have been having these problems for a year now."

"What kind of problems?"

"Well, you know," and he paused again, trying to find the right words. "It happens when we make love. I come as soon as I'm inside her. She has no chance for her own orgasm. She's real demanding and for a long time she'd say "I hate you, I hate you, you less than a man." And it made me feel bad, so one day I called over Tony, the boy next door, and explained things to him."

"Where's Tony now?"

"He moved with his family to Baytown, Texas. His father got a job with an oil firm."

"And?"

"Well, Tony would sort of warm her up. Know what I mean?"

"I got the picture. Warm her up."

"Then, at the right time I take over and make her feel good. Understand what I mean?"

So I was supposed to be the ole warmer-upper. I guess I should have jumped at the chance. I mean here was a once in a lifetime deal to score with no strings attached.

People dream of such things. Oh, I had the chance before. The sad young marrieds with three children, next door to my parents' house. 1966. The bone-thin wife Laura came to the fence while I was sun-bathing in the backyard that summer—came in tears saying how Fred had gone out to get drunk and pick up women. Eighteen I was. Embarrassed at the size of my small root half-hidden in hair, the root my father washed for me when we bathed together in my early days, when there was no hair there, and I would wonder why my father had hair. So, Laura's husband Fred left her for the whole day and night, carousing only God knows where, and she crying at the fence, and I patting her hands saying, It'll work out,

Laura, believe me. The three girls tugging at her faded bathrobe, saying this is my momma, and jealous of me. Sure she could have put the kids to bed. Maybe all she wanted was for me to hold her, but then again I figured she wanted me to be her pirate landing in the night. And I couldn't. I mean, all the cars Fred and I washed and worked on together, and the times we went bowling, and fishing, and lifted weights. Would he have understood if he found out? And that went on the whole summer, his getting drunk, and leaving her for days at a time. But I just couldn't take her to bed. Oh, I don't think Fred would have threatened me with his .38, but he would have been hurt. So I wound up just talking to Laura at the fence, her faded housecoat almost always unbuttoned, waiting for me.

But now. Here was this man practically begging me. Who would be hurt? Nobody, I thought. So why shouldn't I?

"She's waiting in bed if you wanna go ahead."

"OK."

"Oh, one more thing. The way I get aroused is by watching you two. But please don't kiss her. That's all I ask. Fondling her is OK, but don't kiss her. Understand?"

"Sure, Cap'n."

We walked into the bedroom together. His wife was already under the sheets. I could imagine her figure, and it was pretty good for her being between 35 and 40. She wore a wig, and her make-up was put on discreetly.

The room was not very dark. The Captain got up to pull the curtains shut. I walked to the corner of the room, unbuckled my pants slowly, then dropped my underwear. I should not have turned around so soon, or at least kept my underpants on before I got in bed, because the Cap'n's wife looks at me naked and begins to laugh uncontrollably.

I felt strange, sort of nervous.

"Ha! Ha! Ha! What are you going to do with *that*?"

The Cap'n, sensing she hurt me, said, "Amy, stop it, stop it right now. You're lucky Kent is doing me this favor."

But she still laughs for a while, and it makes me angry. A stiff beam of sunlight came through the crack in the curtains. You could see the specks of dust in the light.

Cap'n Peck was silent.

I was furious at this hysterical woman, so I ran to the bed and said, "I'll show *you*."

It must have taken a few minutes for her to stop laughing and begin enjoying me. Then she begs me to stay, running her fingers through my hair. I don't remember how long it took, but I felt that great explosion coming on.

Cap'n Peck was ready, so we changed places. I really don't want to say any more about it. I put on my clothes and immediately went to the kitchen. I heard them saying lousy things to each other. She started laughing again, screaming *Tony, Tony*.

I felt strange, asking myself what good did I do anyway, when Cap'n Peck stuck his head through the door and put a twenty dollar bill in my hand. "Thanks, Kent. Everything worked out. See you sometime later. Keep in touch."

I felt pain between my legs, but I knew why, so I tried to forget it. Even as I walked out the front door, I could hear Mrs. Peck laughing.

6.

Dear Reader, my escapade with Amy Peck was only a fantasy. I mean it could have happened, but it never did.

I'm sorry.

And I am not proud of a belly that slides as mine slides. But it could be worse. The man next door, for instance, just survived a plane crash his wife and child didn't survive. In the morning I see him water his flowers and think of nothing to say. If it would not be out of place, I would pat him on the back, tell him I loved his wife dearly, offer to cook his supper, take him to a movie. But I don't. I can only smile faintly, thrust my arm in the air, open-palmed, go about my business. And somehow it matters if he understands me or not. My father says: "Give it time. In a few weeks things will be different."

7.

Steve Smith, who owes me a thousand bucks, and Mary Lamont, who after seven years, could still tickle me with the rub of love — I bet neither of you knows what a picaresque novel is, nor even care. Nor even a *Bildungsroman*. Would you understand that if you gave me money and love I'd write the best picaresque novel you ever read?

Have you ever heard of Goethe, or Henry Fielding, or Thomas Mann? But I forgive you. I am not a wholly unkind man. Or else why would I think of you now, if I were some tyrant? You think I'm crazy? No, not crazy, just lonely.

I am copying certain phone numbers from my old book of numbers into my new book. Certain people stay and certain people go. You Steve and you Mary would be in the book if I had any information on you. But others. I've either lost track of them, or they can teach me nothing now I don't already know. What I'm saying is they've told me all their stories, and thus have been exhausted as resources.

It is midnight. There is a person in this book I haven't called in ages. So I dial. Ten rings I give it and decide no one's home. No wonder: it's so nice out I, too, should be somewhere but here.

There is a woman I know and want to get to know better. But I can never get in touch with her. Whenever I call her at work, she's either in a business meeting or on the phone long distance. And she hardly ever goes home, but rather goes to play tennis. She is divorced and has three children, all of whom are impolite to me when they answer the phone.

I call. "Hello, this is Kent. Is your mother home?"

"Yes, but she's taking a bath."

I would leave a message. However, she's known not to return my calls.

"OK. I'll call back later." I give her twenty minutes and read awhile in a book about Scott Fitzgerald and Zelda.

"Hello, is your mother out of the tub?"

"Yes, but she's gone."

I don't want to ask "where to" because I did that once before, and the teenage girl said I was annoying her by checking up on her mother.

When I saw this lady, Annette, on the street, she said: "You know my daughter tells me you're constantly asking where I am."

"First of all, she's full of crap," I say. "And furthermore I don't give a fuck where you are."

She was speechless.

Maybe I shouldn't have been so blunt, but this woman is really impossible. I think I'll move on to newer and better women.

Chapter Three

1.

When I walk in the Rusty Nail, I can see the glow of the TV, its sound turned up loud, so the large number of people there are able to hear the sportscaster call the play-off game. I'm always interested in football whenever and wherever, but now I see Raindrinker sitting at the far end of the bar. I nudge my way through the crowd, who let out a big yell as the favorite team of most of them scores a touchdown. Raindrinker is sitting quiet and alone, not even interested in the ballgame, a dozen roses next to him.

I wave half way over to him. "Mr. Raindrinker!"

"Soileau!" he replies.

Then he asks me if I want to go out to the back patio, without all the noise. He takes his roses and a Guiness Stout and I order a Guiness, too, and we find ourselves sitting at a wooden table with wooden chairs, away from all the hubbub.

"What's new, fella?" I ask.

"I'm getting married next week."

"And the roses?"

"They're for my fiancée's birthday today. You see, the

roses complement the alcohol here, both being intoxicants, the rose a gift to the soul, the beer a gift to the body. We love to give each to friends and lovers, and our giving is a beautiful thing. The rose's petals are bundled up like so much money, which it spends in its lifetime while withering and dying. But the rose's existence is endless because it can give birth to others as we can. Do you agree, Kent?"

"Yeah, if it weren't destructive, I'd pluck each petal and count them. I'd guess there'd be as many petals as years in someone's long life, maybe eighty or so." There was a long silence as we both thought about what we said. Then I say: "Anyway, congratulations. Are you gonna have a church wedding?"

"Naw, we agreed, since both of us did that already, we'd just have a small civil ceremony. A coupla my old friends will be there. A coupla hers."

"Where did you two meet?"

"I folded a balloon for her son, she asked if we could meet for coffee, and when neither of us could quit thinking about the other, we knew it was time."

"So she has a son from a previous marriage?"

"Uh huh, he's seven now. My own first marriage ended a few years ago with us having no children."

"Care for another Guiness?" I ask.

"Sure. Thanks."

I make my way back to the bar. Suddenly everyone has gotten quiet, then one guy says, "Hit the bastard again." Apparently two guys from opposing teams have just gotten into a scuffle, and everyone on the playing field, including the officials, are trying to break it up. It's pretty funny, cause one official runs up to the brawl at the same time as a padded player, they bump, the official goes down, losing his cap, but gets back up as if nothing has happened. My guess is when they determine who threw the first punch, that guy's gonna get fined a huge amount of money, which is the way they handle things in the NFL: hit you hard in the pocket book. Before long the officials have gotten everything back to normal. They resume play. For awhile, however, the bar crowd has a lively discussion about what just happened.

Raindrinker and I sit, drink and talk for another half hour, then my friend says he has to go home to put the roses in a vase of water. We're both a little tipsy and agree to catch the streetcar. Outside there are two homeless guys staggering across the street, their beer bottles in their hands. Then one of them—I see this clearly and with a slight shock—walks right in front of an oncoming car which hits him, only after its brakes have squealed. He now lies sprawling in the middle of the street. The driver is pissed, gets out, and says, "What are you crazy or something, jumping off the curb like that?" His anger quickly subsides, seeing the man is injured, and he yells out over to the bar: someone call an ambulance! Football or no football, the bar empties of its inhabitants come out to look, and before long the ambulance arrives along with the police. The victim is quickly attended to, put into the ambulance by the paramedics, as the vehicle drives off to the hospital. A burly policeman starts questioning the drunk friend of the victim.

"Yeah," says the friend, "he told me, before he jumped in front of the car, that he didn't want to live anymore."

The next day I read about the whole thing in the section of the papers containing local news. It said the man struck by the oncoming car was in "stable condition" at the Hospital of New Orleans, and his friend as well as the car's driver were taken to Orleans Parish Headquarters, further questioned, and then released. A few weeks later I heard that with only a broken leg and having regained consciousness, the desperate man was given back to the streets he inhabited. I guess he didn't get his wish, not this time anyway.

It's three days now since I've seen Annette. She's just invited me over for supper. What I said before when I was angry with her: don't believe it. Sometimes I'm just all mouth. I really don't hold grudges, and that's one thing I like about myself. So just forget I called Annette impossible. Probably before long the kids will get to like me. Soon it'll be one of the boys' birthday. I think I'll give him a present. Nothing really expensive. Rather something to let him know I'm really not such a bad guy.

This morning my alarm stunned me. My eyes weren't even open yet. I asked myself: who am I? Then: where am I? I looked around my room. It was familiar enough. But was this where I fell asleep? Perhaps someone moved me. I distinctly remember going to sleep 200 miles from here in my grandmother's feather bed, which seemed to float me. My name still wasn't clear. Slowly I remembered: Kent. What about the last name? I knew it was a French name, Louisiana French. I could think of other French names: Savant, Hébert, Ardoin, Thibodeaux, Bertrand, but that's all. It was hot. I got up to turn on the fan. Then it came: Soileau. I finally had it.

Awake I feel I'm still asleep. It is as if there were one of me here and another of me some place else. Stunned, dazzled by the bright, hot morning, I go to my desk and jot down this poem. It is a summer day in winter, not unusual for New Orleans. "Dream Sequence" I'll call it.

> *I'm looking for water.*
> *A stick leads the way.*
> *Out here the land is dry.*
> *There is the flesh*
> *of rabbit somewhere near.*
> *The hawk knows this*
> *as it descends cautiously,*
> *and, sensing me,*
> *soars back again.*
> *All this is very clear.*
> *I try to break the prison*
> *of my sleep, but something*
> *won't let me. Is there*
> *someone here in the room?*
> *I want to tell you my story!*
> *On the roof I hear rain drops*
> *one by one by one.*

Actually I should feel incredibly lucky that my father still lets me live in the same house with him. Some sons leave at eighteen, some twenty-one, some twenty-five. But twenty-nine! Yes, I should feel lucky, though I've lived in other places in my life, and I'm quite capable of taking care of my own needs. So why did I come back? I'm not sure. I think it was to watch my mother slowly die, to be a witness of losing someone dear to me.

Each day of her life now she goes from bed to kitchen half a dozen times a day. Her cheeks are puffed from the medicine she takes. Her hair is almost always disheveled.

In bed she says again and again: Daddy, Daddy,

Daddy, calling out for my father who is at work across town. Mabel, a black lady from McComb, Mississippi, takes care of her during the day. Mabel has to watch her, to help her from bed to toilet, from bed to kitchen, where she chain smokes cigarettes and stares into space. Once my mother, who can barely lift her arms anyway, dropped a lit cigarette on her woolen slippers. It caught fire, but Mabel put it out. What I can't understand is why my father doesn't put her in an old folks' home. He tells me the doctor doesn't think any place will accept her. Not so much that she's living only on half a liver, rather that she's psychotic complicates things.

It's funny. I thought my father would go before my mother. As a young man, he had rheumatic fever and was bed-ridden for months. The doctors then, in World War Two, all told him he'd have heart trouble before he was forty-five. Now he's fifty-six, still healthy, not looking a day over forty-five. I pretty much love my father. All he asks is that I help him do the things he can't, his having to stay with my mother when Mabel goes home. Things like grocery shopping, going to the drug store, going to the bank. And I have time to do these things since I'm working part-time only, sometimes helping my friend Bill at his print shop, and sometimes working as a page in a library. I decided against the galley hand job offshore I was telling Cap'n Peck about. First of all, my brother tells me, they fly you out in the Gulf in helicopters. I like airplanes, but not helicopters. Then they work you twelve hours a day for anywhere from two weeks to a whole month straight. My brother worked out there for a while.

I might as well tell the story he told me. Decide for yourself if it's worth it.

The drilling rig, a big floating tub's all it is. All night

long the sound of motors humming and fans turning somewhere. The morning goes fast. Then it's afternoon.

The cook, a very heavy, round man, has been saying stuff like (to the man who just picked up a medium rare steak) "Go tell 'em where you got it and how easy it was to git." And now, while I'm chopping up lettuce and tomatoes for a salad, that heavy, round man tells me: "Yep, I treat them guys out here like gods. I give 'em burnt offerings three times a day." Well, that last comment has me in pain with laughter.

"Gosh, David," he says, "it doesn't take much to amuse you."

I have been out here at the Ocean Traveler drilling rig for three days as a galley hand, and I may not last long. I've been cleaning toilets, urinals, making beds, washing dishes, cleaning pots, mopping, moping, sweeping, making coffee and tea, and helping that round heavy man named Clyde. The workers just call him Cook. We stay here two weeks at a time. New oil crews are coming in every week, so we have to keep learning new names or no names at all. Mostly there are picky redneck and Cajun welders who'll hate you if you don't make their coffee fresh every three hours. Fresh and strong. To make weak coffee means they'll be out to get you in a poker game.

The helicopter ride out here was bumpy. Took an hour from shore. The thing vibrated so much you couldn't hear the guy next to you unless you shouted. The cook sat next to me. He could see I was fidgety, always looking around. Basically I dislike these egg beaters. Look at them and you wonder how they fly at all. Some guys sleep in flight. Not me. If that lone pilot needs something, I want to be awake to know about it.

Yes, we're out here, a hundred miles from Grand

Chenier, Louisiana, 275 feet above the floor of the Gulf of Mexico. The cook and I share the same cabin. And it is only a cabin. Not big enough for a room. We talk about lots of things. You don't get much for your money any more. We're underpaid as usual. Black folks? Sundays at church they dress up better than white folks. They keep the cleaners in business. If they can't pay this week, it'll be next week. But the heavy man here will get it. He used to own a cleaners. He knows. Black folks in Opelousas gave him most of his business. Black folks in the country wear woolens even in summer, so they're good customers.

The cook's brother is in Africa drilling for oil. His daddy was a driller too. In the late seventies a house is a good investment. The cook has one of his own in Opelousas. I don't worry about it much, owning a house. A lot of trouble, if you ask me.

A helicopter crashed last year only seven minutes away from the rig. Our heavy cook and his galley hand were supposed to be on that helicopter, but they stopped for a beer and missed it. They are thankful for their lives.

My brother told me all this, more or less, in a letter which my mother opened a few weeks ago. My mother and I never have conversations. She has to strain to talk. Sometimes she'll say, barely audible and with effort: "Do you remember when you were little and...." The rest I can't understand.

There's lots of things I always wanted to tell my mother, but really couldn't. For instance: if you're a guy never ask your friends to fix you up with a girl. If they know a girl, or several, they're probably sleeping with them and don't want to lose a good thing. You can't even ask a friend politely, "Could you fix me up?" He'll just think what a loser you are with women. No, sir. I haven't seen many single or divorced guys I know who are matchmakers. They want the pie for themselves. I musta tried calling up this one friend fifteen or twenty times. Each time he says: "I really haven't seen the girl you want to meet for a long time now." Or: "You know, Kent, the girl I had in mind for you just got married." It's sad, sad.

2.

Really I can't complain. They let me go early today from the library. Upset stomach. Felt like it'd all come up if I stayed around. The job's pretty dull: shelving books the kids come in and take off the shelf and put back in the wrong places. But the boss is no slave driver. He likes to goof off too. My head full of poems. Like I said, I can't complain.

The wind had picked up as I pulled out of my parking space. Before I got in the car I felt my shoes stepping on the very bottoms of my pants and pulled them up over my belly that slides. I thought about my childhood, shoes coming untied, and stepping on the pants' leg, which was too long and would get caught in the inside of my shoe. I was doing it again, sort of.

No traffic going home. The wind picking up in early February. Perhaps a storm's on the way. My car backfires, leaks oil. The windshield wipers strain to work, and there's a crack across the whole length of the windshield. I don't know when I'll get it fixed. Maybe I'll have enough saved in six months. Maybe not.

Home now, I open the back door. It sticks. This land used to be a pig farm and a dump back in the late forties. Whenever it's dry out, the door sticks. When it rains, the door comes unstuck. The ground swells and unswells here like a belly.

Father's in the kitchen feeding my mother. "Put that damn cigarette out," he tells her. A bite of food. A drink through a straw. Another bite of food.

I'm on a diet now. For twenty-nine years I always thought I'd be skinny Soileau. My meal tonight: whole chicken breasts, the bone removed. Expensive.

I open the refrigerator, pull out the chicken breasts with no bones, take the skin off. My father hasn't said a word up till now.

"Have to spend money on expensive meat?" he asks. "I paid your life insurance again this month."

"I'm on a diet."

"Damn it, you'll never learn, will you?"

"Dad, I'm twenty-nine," I wanted to say. "First you tell me, 'well, I was never fat at your age.' Now you won't let me eat what I want to lose weight." But I never said any of it.

"Just like black people," he continued. "Get a dollar in your pocket and you have to spend it on the most expensive thing."

" 'Black people, like black people,' that's all I hear! Don't you think you're being a little hypocritical? You forget your father sharecropped — in the nineteen thirties — with one of those people who became a famous accordion player of *la musique créole*, and we go to visit with him whenever he plays at festivals."

He scoops the mashed up yams and red beans into my mother's mouth.

"Father," I wanted to say, "don't take your bitterness out on me. You brought me into this world." But I said this instead: "I refuse to talk to you unless you let me live the way I've learned I must live." My father did not speak.

Sometimes he is the type of man who holds grudges.

3.
Some almost final words to Annette. The death of a phone. Annette's mishaps.

Monday night I call Annette. Her eight-year-old answers the phone. I try to talk about the weather, how he is doing, anything. "I don't know," he keeps answering all my questions pertaining to his welfare. Then he becomes entirely monosyllabic. I am crushed, though perhaps I shouldn't be.

Tuesday night I call again. I let the phone ring 47 times. There is no answer. Wednesday night, the same. All phone calls have been made at seven PM, a time when reasonable people are usually at home. Now for two weeks, no Annette, no children at seven PM. Where can they have gone?

Time for revenge. Yes, I will stay up till two in the morning for this. After all, the whole lousy family must sleep some time.

2 AM. I only imagine: I call. A groggy voice answers hello. I hang up. I do this five times each night for two weeks straight. And I only imagine: Annette and her family must have decided to get an unlisted number by now. They must be tired of all the late night calls, where the caller says nothing and hangs up. I imagine: I call their old number once more, but a disembodied voice tells me it's been disconnected.

I don't know why, but after all this imagining, I decide to write Annette a cordial letter.

```
Dear Annette MacDonald,
```

(Her last name must be used here to put some distance between us.)

After spending a night of serious
thinking and much grief, I have
decided to break off all relationships
which are detrimental to my well-
being. I am weeding out the garden of
my life.

Communication with you has proved
futile. I am forever talking to your
children, who fail to relay messages
to you, and who greet me with little
respect and less enthusiasm.

I have also decided that the telephone
is a monstrously unkind beast and
should be shot. If I have any dealings
with anyone any more, I want to
see them face to face. I make long
distance phone calls to friends, and
it gets me nowhere. I make calls to
you which are in vain. I feel I must
find someone I can see on a day to
day basis, who can at least give the
pleasures of conversation and the
sweetness of a face.

And so what more can I say but
goodbye? If I seem miserly or unkind
in any way, I'm sorry, but I have
learned how I must live my life, and I

shall live it that way.

        Sadly,
        Kent Soileau

Two days later Annette calls me up. "Can we meet at Big Johnny's Pizza Place on Elysian Fields tonight at seven? I got your letter, and I'm sorry."

"Sure," I say. I am not a hard man. I am no longer angry.

Over a few beers, and she is confiding in me as never before. Softly she tells me how her ex-husband had a small penis. When he was in the service, he was too embarrassed to take a shower with the others. Why, they had only one position in bed that worked, his penis was so small. Five years after the divorce, on the night of his daughter's birthday, he came back home nearly a thousand miles and demanded sex, though she said "absolutely not" and "you have some nerve." She is silent for a long time.

I think: who can preach to the sky when even the trees won't listen? There are no hurrahs here for the trees' impatience with the wind, for the wind's anger from June to September when finally fathers board their houses, knowing that nothing is safe from a hurricane. In 1965, for Hurricane Betsy, when the water rose up past the top of our door sill and ruined all the furniture, small boys paddled small boats down the river which was our street. And they were happy. Two days later the water went down, leaving the stench of dead eels on everyone's front lawn.

I think, too, of moths fluttering in one place, unable to fly, of bones in a child's leg that will never straighten no matter how many times you invoke the stars.

And I know, listening to Annette tell me that today she was fired from her job, that neither of us are done with our changes.

As for the telephone, I'm still sick of it, that hermaphroditic beast that craves for attention always by sounding its distress call of bells. Yes, the telephone wants to be rescued again and again. You can almost hear it cry "wolf" with each ring. By the time it has rung you wrong for the sixth time in an hour, it has become a liar and a cheat.

Case in point: my brother's future wife has called six times this morning getting me out of bed and sweet dreams each time. It is Saturday morning. They live together in Poydras, Louisiana about twenty miles from here, and he comes home on the weekend. This woman calls him six times, not even giving him a chance to get home. Every call: is David there? Tell him it's important. Tell him to call me. I'm tired of this psychotic bitch waking me up, and on the seventh phone call from her, I can't hold it in any longer. I have to raise my voice and say: "Would you please quit calling here? Shit!" And slam down the phone. I am convinced. Telephones belong to lonely, weak people. People afraid to get in their cars or walk over to a neighbor's house and simply knock. People who can't live unless they have instant gratification. But enough preaching.

I know I'll have to answer to my father for this, cause it's his phone, but it's something I must do. My father has a sledge hammer in the garage. I get it. I take the telephone out to the brick patio in the backyard. My two dogs are barking. They see me raise the hammer. They sense my anger. Run around to the other side of the house. It's time. Somehow this whole thing is even a challenge, like making the bell ring with a hammer at an amusement park. Here my only prize will be peace of mind. I let the hammer fall three times. I remember how my grandfather had to smash the heads of six puppies which were starving. He did it behind his barn where he thought no one would see. But I saw. At ten years old I saw. And now I feel like the first pioneer who drove a stake where his house would be built on the prairie. The bell on the phone rings as I smash it. Pieces of plastic, thousands of them, fly in a thousand different directions. The next day my father asks what happened to the phone, it is not in the room. "I don't know, Dad, it must've exploded or somethin'." The conversation doesn't end here. It's sad, sad.

Another pertinent story, however, about Annette. You, Reader, decide. Annette knows the owner of the Peach Tree. It's a coffeehouse on Prytania uptown. Annette usually spends Thursday nights talking with her. When I called, the person who answered said *hold on* before I could say anything. I musta waited for about five minutes. Then someone says: "Who ya waitin' for?" "Annette. Is she there?" "OK" and I heard the receiver hit something. I hate it when life is so impersonal. What did that guy care? For five minutes I listened to loud juke box music in the background, afraid that if I took my ear away from the receiver, Annette might answer. She never answered. Somebody finally hung up the phone. She never answered.

Annette is having an awful time of it lately. A week ago she was disco dancing with some guy. When he spun her around, she tripped and his elbow hit her right in the eye. (Serves her right for ignoring me so much.) Now she tries to cover that plum-purple bruise with make-up. Then, two nights ago, her lesbian friend Marina (they're just friends) hit her above the left eye, leaving a bruised bump there. All of Marina's movements are histrionic—because she feels people think she's ugly—and she always tends to rush everything. This time she was handing a Coke bottle to Annette like an actress in a sweeping gesture. She smacked her. Then last night playing tennis Annette tore two ligaments in her ankle, and now she has to limp around. The doctor said it wasn't serious enough to operate. Annette is now breaking off her relationship with Marina, ever since Marina told Annette she was in love with her. But the main reason is that Marina is so prone to cause accidents. Last month Marina took Annette and her children for a simple drive in the park and ran into a tree.

Last night I dreamed that Marina tried to kill herself by lighting her body doused with gasoline. It was windy. The match kept going out. Finally lightning struck. She went up in flames. She decided she didn't want to die after all, so she started rolling on the ground to put out the flames. There was a cliff's edge nearby, and she rolled herself off the cliff, falling thousands of feet.

4.

Borrowing

1. I can't believe it. My brother has the nerve to look me in the eye, knowing he has owed me four dollars for three months now. I don't speak to him. He knows it, and yet he continues to not even give me some idea when he will pay me back. My sister found out he lost his good job, and is now working for minimum wage as a security guard. No excuse. He still owes me four dollars.

2. It's break time at my new job at the library (another

library). I want to read poems, but the lady wants to talk politics. Ten years ago, to Rafael Smith, my college roommate, I would have stared him in the face and mumbled: "I don't want to talk politics, ever."

But it is now. I just sit and politely listen to this lady who keeps giving details about things even when you haven't asked her for details, even when she is borrowing my time.

I'm thinking how last Saturday, the whole day I'd thought it was Sunday, till at night driving along the highway, I saw the shops lit up for business, and knew only then it was Saturday.

Pretty soon I'm going to have to say no to Tyronne. He works with me at the library. For the last month he's been borrowing a quarter from me every week. "Say man," he says, "you have a quarter? I'll pay you back tomorrow." He may really need it, but so do I. He looks down with his brown puppy's eyes every time he asks. But he'll never pay me back, I just know it. I'm such a nice guy. Just because I talk to him, he begs.

Every morning he reads the sports' page. He comes in early and sits in the lounge with a cup of coffee. You think he cares about the English professor who is going to prison for razoring out five thousand dollars' worth of maps in the rare book room of the Yale library? Probably not. I care. I had this same professor for an English course, once. I'm wondering what he's going to do when he gets out. He's lost his job. Who will hire him now? Perhaps he is contemplating suicide even now.

Thinking about Tyronne also reminds me of the dollar a childhood friend borrowed on his sixteenth birthday in 1966, and I still haven't seen it.

3. I remember an unshaven young man on Canal Street held a knife to a dog's head. He said to me: if you don't give me a dime, I'll have to eat this dog. Nearby street people were selling a pile of underground newspapers they took out of a vending machine when a citizen dropped a quarter in it.

5.

Bert

Driving today I saw the shadow of a helicopter cross the highway, and I began to think: I suppose I'm the one to blame for Bert's disappearance. My sister has been in tears on and off since Sunday when we found a dog-sized hole burrowed under our wire fence. As for me, I can't cry. Sure, I liked Bert, but maybe someone picked him up and is giving him a pretty good home.

Sunday the thunderstorms came. Bert hated them. His whole body would tremble if he sensed one coming, and he would crouch into himself and look for shelter. When we first got Bert years ago, my father heard him scratching at the breezeway door in the presence of a storm. So he nailed a small piece of rubber, big as a shoe heel, to the door. Bert learned to bite it and open the door as soon as he heard thunder. After two years of this I knew Bert would seek shelter for the rest of his life. On Sunday I thought I'd teach him a lesson: I nailed the breezeway door shut so he couldn't come in. Later, no one had seen Bert the whole day. We found the hole dug under the fence. I drove to the animal shelter to see if the dog catcher had picked him up. No luck. My sister ran an ad in the paper offering a reward. No one called. Perhaps Bert is in the Kingdom of Dog. Oh, Bert, how many times has the body observed itself, as if in the front of its own mirror, solitary, stiffening, triumphant, and in Hinduism anyway, knowing it may be whole again, but never the same.

6.

Each night the moon turns orange the golden Chinaberry tree whispers that it, too, cannot remember names, and that comforts me. February and already the dogs drink less, and the moths keep vigil another season. This winter I will have quiet because I will ask for it. I will ask trees, beasts—morning, I will say, don't be so restless. Wind, I will say, anger helps no one. Noon, I will say, vengeance is cruel. Father, I will say, a poet once said patience is everything.

My feet are flat like my mother's, my eyes are each a different color, and perhaps I am not the man my mother wanted me to be. In my childhood I have survived being thrown from a horse twice in the same day, a mad friend pointing a gun at me, seven stitches after having accidentally slit my wrist with a milk bottle, broken while I washed dishes and shook it so that it hit the side of the sink. I have survived fifteen-year-olds wanting me to break in a locked school building, wanting me to steal cars, wanting me to smoke. And yet I am still not successful, and don't really want to be, though someday I want to be a modest molecular geneticist. Such are the thoughts recorded by Kent Soileau on a late-winter afternoon nearing his twenty-ninth spring, having ended his relationship with Annette MacDonald thus:

"Annette, I'm sorry I wrote you that nasty note, but I was in love with you."

"I think I must have hurt you before. It's over, Kent."

"Then I want my typewriter back."

"Aha, so it wasn't a gift, after all."

"It was, but you're being such a turd about this whole thing."

"OK. I'll leave the typewriter in your driveway. I don't want you coming to my house." And then she hung up; for one week I planned killing her, egging her car, writing "Death to All Weirdos" on the driver's window where she'd see it. But I did nothing. Now I'm hopeful more women will come into my life. It's sad, sad. I don't mean the new women. I mean my feelings about Annette.

It's been a long week. I need a beer and someone to talk to about losing Annette.

Guess who pops into my mind? Raindrinker. As I expected, he's at the Rusty Nail again. He tells me he understands how I feel, since even he and his wife are having spats, and he, too, needs a beer whenever she yells at him. It's almost closing time on a Tuesday night, and the two of us are the only customers. Buddy the bartender has been pacing up and down, talking to himself, squinting his eyes, and twitching his head. "Could ya quit with the pacing, Buddy?" I say. "Hell, you're making me nervous." Either he doesn't hear me, or he doesn't want to hear me cause he keeps doing what he was doing before I said anything.

Raindrinker says, "I was summoned today for possible jury duty. There musta been twenty people waiting to be questioned by attorneys for a criminal case. They paid you three whole dollars for the afternoon. But I specified on my form that my three dollars go to the Parish Child Welfare Board."

"A noble gesture on your part, my good man."

He continues, "It was a second offense DWI case. Prosecutors and defense attorneys asked us a bunch of questions about what we thought the law meant when it said "willful and wanton" drunk driving, and would we trust a cop's testimony, and so forth. I felt a part of something our forefathers gave us. Since I didn't want to run for office (one way to participate in representative government), I could also either vote or be a jury member. But I told the defense guys there is a pattern of behavior I saw in my uncle's drunken driving that he would never give up. So I'm sure because of that, having a bias against drunk drivers, I was not chosen. Also, get this, the attorney asked if we thought just one drink would impair our driving ability. And I said, I don't know, is it a double? And laughed. Which drew a couple of laughs from my peers, but didn't seem to go well with the attorneys who kind of frowned. Aw, fuck 'em if they can't take a joke. Well, that little slip of the tongue cost me my first chance to be a juror."

"Well, you gave it your best shot."

"Right. But had I been a juror, I would have learned a good bit about those who inhabit this earth with me."

"Ah, but you can learn that by just coming to a bar."

"Sure. Also you can learn good jokes to keep your friends laughing."

"Raindrinker, sometimes you amaze me. Would you teach me how to fold balloons?"

"Ah, my friend, that's a secret. That's what makes me the magician I am."

7.

Early March. The rain began to fall heavy in the last light of afternoon. The wind and clouds came quickly, and not until the first drops did I realize I had at least half a lawn more to cut. I was using an old gasoline mower. Something must have been wrong with it: it speeded up and slowed down in an endless cycle. But it cut the grass well enough. There was no need to have it fixed.

My brother sits on the front steps watching me. He's been away from home for a month now living with the girl he'll marry as soon as her divorce goes through. We didn't get along very well when he lived at home with me. At best I tolerated him, occasionally telling him my stories and troubles. But now he steps off the front porch into the rain and says hello.

"Where ya been keepin' yourself?" I ask.

"Oh, around."

"Anything new with you?"

"Yeah, Nora and I are going to have a baby."

"Great. You know, it's really good to see you."

"Good to see you too."

"You don't mind getting wet?"

"Oh no. It's sorta fun really."

"David, what are you going to tell the baby when it grows up?"

"The truth, I guess, that Nora and I really loved each other when the baby was conceived." He adds, "The other night she let me feel it kicking."

I knew he was happy. But to tell the truth I had no feelings about it one way or the other. I want to have a child someday. Still, I am not moved even when my brother tells me he will. In fact, people will be all excited about such things, and most of them don't realize that having babies increases the anxiety in the parents.

By the time I finish the lawn, we're both wet. Nora pulls up in the driveway. She's just back from picking up her child by her first marriage from a nursery. At first I didn't like Nora. I'd even avoid talking to her. But now I know she's made a commitment to David, I feel a lot better about her. (My brother is consistently attracted to married women with children, just as once, for five years, I was attracted to short blondes.)

Two days ago I trimmed the hedges, and some of the leaves fell on my neighbor's side of the fence. I see in the meantime he's raked them up. His door opens. He shouts over to me: "Hey, fella, I'm gonna pick a fight with you. You know I cleaned up the mess you left."

"Sorry, Mr. Streiten, I meant to."

"That's OK, I'll send you my bill."

And he closes his door. He doesn't mean anything by his replies. He is serious only about one-fourth the time.

My brother takes a shower, dries up. Then he and Nora and little Cindy go inside to talk with my sister and father. I'm not a real talker when it comes to the family sitting around the kitchen table so I go to my room and listen to the record I've learned to like, the record I listen to every afternoon about this time again and again.

8.

Oh, Turgenev, the way you composed your characters, especially Bazarov in *Fathers and Sons*, still amazes me. Where are the Bazarovs of today? I wish you were here to guide my pen. Then, after a writing session, I'd treat you to breakfast: scrambled eggs, grits, and pork sausage. Ivan, I think you would see the world different now. What I want to say is this: character is no longer everything. There are no more color portraits drawn every few months or years throughout the character's life. There are only brief sketches, and even those are incomplete. Do you doubt that I have the talent to create well drawn characters? I don't know. But it wouldn't be honest. Still, know that the smoke from the fire of your prose stings my eyes, and tears come like a new mother's. So it is truly what Rilke said in a letter to Franz Kappus: everything is gestation and then bringing forth. You may not have to be reminded of that. I, however, think of it always.

Thank you. Sincerely, Soileau. The 4th of March, the day of my mother's birth, fifty-six winters ago, when, like now, her legs were drawn to her chest.

Chapter Four

*An Interview With My Father In the Living Room
He's Dozed Off In For Thirty Years*

Why did I believe everything in 1955?
    —You were young, a fine boy.

Why could my short pants have hung from a dog's tail?
    —You were wise, intelligent, full of energy and good
bones.

**Would you play the home movie backwards again?
I want to see the food at the barbecue come out of my
mouth back onto the fork, and the splash of water return
to itself as I rise like an angel to the diving board.**
    —Sure. Just let me focus. There!

**I remember driving with you on a four hour trip to
Grandmother's house, with Mother and Brother in the
back seat, me in the front, and you driving. How did you
feel when I went to sleep? I fell asleep easy. It was the
hum of the car on the road.**

—I didn't want you to sleep. I wanted somebody to talk to besides the radio. I guess at heart I was a lonely man.

Is that why I saw your head hang down as you sat in the yard, having put together 2x4's for a day's worth of building a garage, the sweat pouring from your face, mother saying to you, "Damn it, get your own iced tea."? Is that why you hung your head down?

—I have forgiven your mother.

Were you ever depressed in your life?

—Never depressed. Lonely.

Were you ever sad?

—I was sad only once or twice. Yes, I was sad when your grandfather lost his arm to dynamite in the fields. But after that I got used to his teasing, poking me in the ribs with that stump of an arm that couldn't hurt a mosquito hawk.

The night Hurricane Betsy came and the roof was starting to lose shingles, and the windows cracked, and the water began to rise, and things were pretty bad, were you afraid?

—No, but it was a fine, hell of a time for you to fall asleep on me.

I'm sorry. But what'd you expect from a listless seventeen-year-old with a crew cut? And that's another thing: why did you want me to wear my hair trimmed practically to the scalp?

—You were a former sailor's son. Your face was made for a crew cut.

And you saved money, of course, cutting my hair yourself. It musta been easy. Zip, zip, and I was bald for all practical purposes.

--But you had a cow lick in the front and back. You were pretty cute. Then you got to be nineteen, wanting to wear your hair long as any hippie. And didn't I let you?

I'm embarrassed. But I'm supposed to ask the questions.

--OK

In most of the pictures around the house I'm always smiling a tiny, pristine smile. Why don't I smile smug and cocky?

--You were never that type.

When I had flat feet at five, you took me to the chiropodist. He put in those arch supporters that were supposed to correct flat feet, only I remember not wanting to wear them. I hated them. Then it was off to the dentist later to straighten the teeth, and later to the dermatologist for the acne. I guess I had it pretty good as a kid.

--Good and expensive.

Did you mind?

--No, and I'll add that psychologists seem to think most kids make it through life OK even in the most adverse circumstances. Of course, some grow up any way they can. Kids do alright for themselves. Your mother worried whether you'd survive. Enh! (shoulder shrug)

There are lots of photographs in the album. There are a few in particular I'd like to ask you about.

--That's a picture of your mother pouting. You know, women didn't do that in the old days when I rode the Oregon Trail and the Chisholm Trail. We cowboys wouldn't put up with that nonsense.

That's pretty funny. Now, as a child in the Catholic Church I felt that when I died a Court of Divine Justice would review films of my whole life and condemn me to Hell for each of my sins. Did you ever think the Church would do that to me?
    --You were pretty tough on yourself. I didn't realize that, no. I can only hope going to church gave you some structure.

You once told me that as a young man you worked in a warehouse where your boss told you: "I'd rather have one experienced man than ten like you."
    —It hurt, yes.

We never had a piano. Who could have ever thought the piano had so many possibilities?
    —That's true. But you had a clarinet and some talent, if only you'd have practiced more. What happened?

Practicing was a chore with all the funny-eyed girls around. Besides, I wanted to be a photographer then.
    —Which you did in high school, but abandoned.

Back to the photo album. Is this the same cat we caught one Thanksgiving morning dragging the turkey across the living room floor, headed for God knows where?
    --The same. He died at the paws of a jealous cat. An honorable way for a cat to die.

Here's me barefooted in the house. Why was that?
—Did you want your feet condemned to the prison of your socks and shoes?

No, that's right. Here's a picture of you as a child. Isn't that fantastic, in sepia? You musta been about ten. What do you guess you were thinking about?
—Arnold Savant stood behind the camera: a dry day, perhaps the moon out. At our thirtieth reunion of the class of '39, Mamou High School, I saw him. He had become a doctor and an alcoholic. He looked twice his age. But we were close friends as children. We both walked two miles to the school bus, a model-A Ford with no windows, just flaps of canvas. Arnold was afraid of thunderstorms, so when it rained hard, he shivered next to me. In the winter the pieces of canvas would flap back and forth. In this picture it is winter. I am thinking, *zéro dans la poussière*, French for "zero in the dust." Arnold and I and a group of boys had played marbles. The teacher had whipped Arnold for speaking Cajun French in class instead of English. We called him "tsee" (*petit*) Arnold because he was smaller than the rest. Anyway, Arnold was losing at marbles, and I took a stick and drew a big zero in the dust. "Zéro dans la poussière" everyone shouted. Arnold, bad luck Arnold, got up, brushed the dust from his pants, and sulked away.

You watch the Lawrence Welk Show every Saturday night. You subscribe to *National Geographic* and *Consumer Reports*. You read the daily newspaper front to back, and your interest is in U. S. History, especially

the history of warfare in the twentieth century. You love Churchill's *History of World War II*. Why these?

—I was born in 1922. Everyone I know who was born about that time watches Lawrence Welk. His music says something to us, its gentleness. It's music with a quiet voice. As for *Geographic*, it is living history. I am an avid consumer. I like to take my time when I buy something that will last and that will cost more money than most other things I buy, hence *Consumer Reports*. I lived the best years of my life during and after the Second World War, and died and came back many times; that is why I love Churchill, a fitting spokesman for the grief of war.

You look like you're asleep. What's wrong?

—I always close my eyes when I'm thinking. And also my eyelashes are straight so people think I'm sleeping whenever they talk to me.

Do you sleep well enough these days with Mother calling out in her need?

—The power of a tomato is surely enough to waken me: ah, the nightmares of tomatoes! Otherwise I've learned to sleep moments at a time. In my sleep I hear your mother calling. When I was young, they could throw a bucket of cold water on me and, if I was in a deep sleep, I would still not wake up.

How many times do you think single women have asked around if you were married? How many times has morning lifted the darkness from your face, taken it unto itself, wakened you?

—Many, many times.

In my life I've seen how I've admired old men because they knew more stories than I did.

—The old man rests in the knowledge that he has lived. Your grandfather, for instance. Look at him in 1967, the year before his death. Though his mind is filled with wilderness, his thoughts, amazingly, come out metered, as though he tames the wilderness of his thoughts. In disorder there is order. If his house, which is his sanctuary, is in disorder, he does not worry. Some time, in good time, he will give it order again, just as spring gives order to winter. And he does not care how he looks. He lets the wind muss his hair if it wants to. He does not ask the love of his grandchildren, only that they let his hand rest for a moment on their heads.

Sometimes I wish I had your ordered thoughts, your impeccable adult ego state.

—Though I anger sometimes, I will try not to force my thoughts on you. You have your own thoughts. But I hope I have taught you to respect the solitary things: our beds, as close to us as our shoes, as close as our lovers, maybe closer, the trees, the seasons, the night which has seasons of its own, the lovely animals, bowing in silence.

Father, what have you seen today?

—Kent, tell me if you've seen it: how a good cigar, never mind the small death of its ashes, will always come back to life.

Chapter Five

✤

1.

They call this the Family Room. I'm alone in here now. The rest are in the main room where the casket is open. So I thought I'd start writing.

It is Monday morning. Mother died Saturday at 7 PM. I had been away at a friend's eating supper. When I got home my sister and my father stared at me. I looked in the bedroom where Mother had been sleeping. There were no sheets on the bed. I thought they had an ambulance take her to the hospital again. But I was wrong. My sister hugged me and whispered the news in my ear. I was not shocked. Only a few minutes later did my eyes water up. But that was all: I had expected the news.

Well, Mother was born in Fusilier, a little town in Evangeline Parish. There was a gas shortage, so we had to wait till Monday morning for the hearse to drive 200 miles to New Orleans and drive her back to Fusilier.

All morning I have been seeing relatives I've not seen in years. The ones who were little years ago have children of their own. And the ones who were middle-aged long ago were mostly overweight (I shouldn't talk) and wearing dentures now.

In the last few years there has been a general decline in wakes. Watching the dead lie horizontally is for many unnecessary and even unbearable. They would rather put the grief of death out of their minds as quickly as possible, let the dead return to the earth as soon as the flesh grows cold. I, for one, think if the deceased has many mourners, give them a chance to renew all friendships, both living and dead.

When I got to the funeral home, my father explained he had selected an inexpensive wooden casket. He said my mother would have found the more expensive metal caskets "tacky." I kneeled at the casket and said a prayer, one of the several I had learned by heart as a child studying in Catechism. I considered myself a lapsed Catholic.

The usual bouquets of flowers were there. Actually they bored me. I'm not one much for flowers. I touched Mother's cold forehead, then stroked her thinning gray hair. So now she was somewhere, she didn't know where, as one who has just been put to sleep on an operating table.

That night when the crowd was largest in the reception room, little groups of folks would occasionally break out in laughter. Tante Ann had her same long, sculptured nose, and her daughters were young and pretty. All the rumors I'd heard about her getting drunk and running around with other men hit me immediately, but I said only: Boy, Ann, it's been a long time. "You can sleep at my house tonight," she said. "Thanks, but I'm staying at Grandma's." She had just bought her daughter a new car. Her rouge was put on a little too heavy.

Parrain Pierre was there. I had written a poem about him. Told him so. He seemed pleased, but couldn't read well, even had I brought along the poem. Perhaps I could have read it to him aloud. He told me about his job. There is always lots to talk about at wakes: new cars, new recipes, new wives, sweet faces, how much the little ones have grown. This bores me less than it used to.

I remember 1954, winter, when the trees stopped whispering, and the clouds gathered in their great darkness, my mother picked me up from my wrecked bicycle on the street, both my legs broken. She held me in her arms and sang me a lullaby of old times. And once, going to Eunice on an old Trailways bus, I said "Momma, I have to wee wee bad." She unzipped my short pants, held my hairless fledgling of a penis, put the cellophane of her cigarette pack between my legs and said: "Let it go, son." Then the cellophane sack filled, and Mother dumped it out the window.

Tonight I have seen women come with walking canes to see my mother for the last time. I have seen men who can hardly breathe come too. The priest walks in now, and the crowded room becomes silent. The priest bows his head and begins: For the First Holy Mystery of the Blessed Virgin. And chants the first half of a Hail Mary while mourners reply with the second half. All over the room prayers echo, and everyone's fingers follow prayer beads around a circle.

Holy Mother, let her find comfort in the tight spaces of the small home she will now inhabit. Let the darkness finally fill the new earth of her body and her shadow finally wrap itself around her. Let her keep the late hour chanting with the dead: "you are alone — we are the ones together." Let her know the sea dark, the wind dry, the air pure. Let her dream the living and let the living dream her.

My love, now you will feel the wind hovering over you, wind that has felt distance, and though it is night for you, it will be night over half the world. This is the prayer of Kent Soileau, who as a lapsed Catholic in his twenty-ninth year will begin the study of the Great Religions of the World. For though he sits in the stillness of things, he cannot yet speak of stillness.

2.

It turns out I had to miss the funeral the next day. In the middle of the night I got sick with what everyone suspected: appendicitis. My father rushed me to the hospital early that morning and left me alone. He asked me if I understood that he had to get back to the funeral mass at nine that morning. I nodded. The doctor gave me an anesthetic about ten or eleven. As far as I can piece things together, just as the funeral director was lowering the casket into the ground on a misty Tuesday morning, the surgeon's clean knife was sliding into the soft, fleshy sponge that was my belly.

3.

Yesterday we got a new phone. My father called the phone company and paid for the one I smashed. I in turn paid him for it. It was a plain, black phone. Which tells you something about him. With him: no fancy phones, no coordinated colors, no push buttons, just plain black. And yet sometimes my father is a whimsical man, light-hearted, responsive, salt of the earth. He is a lot like John Carroll, especially at the end of that John Wayne movie, *The Flying Tigers*. In fact, my father even looks like John Carroll with his moustache.

Anyway, John Wayne has some nitroglycerine aboard a DC-3, ready to fly in low to blow up a bridge that is the enemy's supply line. John Carroll as Woody is the happy-go-lucky, but often careless mercenary who is responsible for most of Wayne's headaches. Woody gets aboard the plane unnoticed by Wayne. Should Wayne keep Woody for the mission, or should he tell him to bail out? "You can stay, Woody," Wayne says finally. Woody replies: "OK, Pappy," waving his hand whimsically, in gratitude, his voice pausing between the "o" and the "k", the "k" said with a falling pitch.

Yes, Friday night the new phone rings for its first time. It's a lady from Dave Breen's headquarters. He's running for governor of Louisiana. She asks me if I want to volunteer my time to help him get elected.

"I'm sorry," I say, "but I'm an anarchist."

"Oh, really?" she asks politely. "What's that? Is that pretty bad?"

Surely I'm no anarchist. I don't even like politics. But somehow I felt it the intelligent thing to do to tell this woman all I knew about anarchism, hoping she would start thinking more seriously about her life. I mean look at Tolstoy. He was an anarchist.

Today I feel good about talking to a stranger. Usually though, when they call asking me to buy subscriptions to magazines to send poor boys to camp, or offer to shampoo my rugs for free with their new and amazing vacuum cleaner, I just say: sorry, I'm not interested.

"To think that anarchism is the same as revolutionary terrorism is a popular misconception. Sacco and Vanzetti were not anarchists. They were perhaps common hooligans who also espoused anarchism, only coincidentally. It is this age of science that makes the unjust social system even worse. We don't need either government or police. What we need is a nation of small communities which co-operate with each other, a kind of trade exchange. Man is infinitely good and can be trusted. Don't you agree?"

"Uh, I guess. But what would you do with all the criminals?"

"Simple. Banish them from society and forbid them to return. There are some tribes in the South Pacific which, in their aboriginal wisdom, do this, and it works for them."

"Say, I have to go now, but thanks for the information," she said, her voice quivering. I bet I scared her off. Oh, well, maybe she'll give her dull life further consideration.

4.

I would give you a tour of my house, though it is not really a house, rather a room. But I must warn you: I am one to reminisce. I have lived here most of the twenty-nine years of my life. If I tell you how an object got here, don't be discouraged. It will be the truth. So this way, please.

You notice the room my father built with the help of no one, my room in the back of the house with its white weatherboards of cypress and yellow awnings and trim; this room, once a garage, is filled with books. Some would call me a capitalist for having so many books. But I must have them close to me, so I can pull them from the shelves. Why buy books? Go to the library, you say? True. I have no answer. Except that I buy very few clothes. I have been fat for quite a while, so years will pass before I buy a new shirt. The heels of my shoes are worn on the outside. What will happen to my books when I enter my next life? At the moment I have no children to bequeath them to. The one *Organic Chemistry*, the one Economics text, the one Contemporary Sociology text, the one called *Choice of a Medical Career*, and all the hundreds of books on fiction, poetry, drama, and literary essays and criticism. If I *am* a capitalist, let the devil take me.

Step this way. Note the trophies. Yesterday I moved them from here to here. I am a compulsive re-arranger. Know this. If I could re-arrange dust, I would. Two dictionaries, both unabridged. *The Jerusalem Bible*, I bought on sale at one-fifth the price. And the books that taught me how to fly a small airplane.

The trophy with the gold officer standing at attention. As much as I would like to throw it away, I can't. The trophy with the golden bowler in his approach, forever holding his ball in a backswing. Yes, I was a pretty good bowler, and I say that modestly.

The thin lines of spider webs that barely make themselves known. The unbelievable sadness of a vacuum cleaner at rest and getting older.

I could tell you so many stories: how I won the trophy with the soldier at attention. Hap Reilly and Dick Mankowitz would know these stories. Gentlemen, are you still out there? Could you vouch for me? In Civil Air Patrol every Friday night we all wore those starched uniforms. And I was a cold officer, once telling a cadet to do twenty push-ups for having a loose thread on his uniform. I ground my shoe into his for not being able to see my face in it. Oh, I was tough. Hap Reilly, whom the children followed around like the President, and Dick Mankowitz, I have gotten soft. I could never be an officer again, even though you gave me that trophy for best drill commander at Summer Encampment, Keesler Air Force Base, in 1967.

Here is my half-filled bottle of cheap whiskey. I give up on it. Here are my pictures at ten, eighteen, and twenty-one in their frames. I give up on them. Here is the globe Father bought me, the countries of Africa all with different names now. Here are the candles, the china ducks in flight, the china frogs. Here is the huge black trunk I never made it to Cincinnati with to study there. Here is one of my favorite slogans, typed by an old Underwood on an index card, and scotch-taped to the wall: Resolve to be tender with the young, compassionate with the aged, sympathetic with the striving, and tolerant of the weak and the wrong. Sometime in life you will have been all of these.

And, by God, I don't even know who wrote it.

5.

Monday night I was watching basketball with my father when the phone rang. I should add that our new phone number was once that of the Pioneer Bus Company. I never heard of it, but lately we've been getting calls asking for information on schedules. One day I looked it up in the Yellow Pages and there it was.

"Pioneer Bus Company?" a girl's voice asked.

"No. This is the Soileau residence."

"Well, I've got to get to Memphis. My mother is driving me mad. Could you drive me up there? I'll pay you fifty dollars. It's all I got. My sister's up there."

"Uh, I'm sorry, but—"

"I think I'm gonna kill myself then."

I knew from an abnormal psych class that treating a suicidal person is risky business for the layman. There are certain things you say and certain things you don't. I must admit I couldn't let this girl go off the deep end.

"Where are you?" I asked.

"A pay phone," she said, her voice shaky.

"Where?"

There was a long silence.

"I'm feeling really depressed now. My mother doesn't understand me." In the background I heard a siren.

"Shit, that bitch must've called the cops on me!"

I heard the receiver hit against something, as if she just dropped it. What can I say? If she'd have told me where she was, I would have gone to talk to her.

I hung up and walked to the den. My father did not volunteer a score, so I asked him. "89-69 Knicks," was all he said, his eyes fixed on the TV. Boston was my team. They were losing to New York. I went to my room. There were only a few minutes left in the game. It looked hopeless for Boston.

I fed the dog, took out the garbage, took a shower, and dried my hair with a blow dryer. I went to my desk but just sat there. What was going on inside me? Was I still wondering about that girl who hated her mother? Was it my childhood? I thought of friends in 1963 who wounded me with their nicknames of me: White-headed Roach and Big Ears. I thought of James Lemoine, who eventually grew to only five feet tall, who squeezed my ear lobes and told me he was milking a cow. Once, me fourteen, James called his gang of boys together into someone's garage, where they felt up the tits of this one girl Sylvia. I just stayed outside and wept for I don't know what. Was it Sylvia?

I couldn't sleep that night, which wasn't unusual. As a child I had asthma and stayed up many nights: lie down and your chest takes on so much weight you can't breathe. This wasn't asthma. I don't know what it was. That made three nights in a row I couldn't sleep. I had never read much of W. H. Auden. So I spent the night going through him. My favorite poem was one he wrote upon the death of Sigmund Freud.

At 5:30 A. M. I decided to balance my check book. At 6 I dressed and had breakfast. Cereal and milk was all there was. Traffic was heavy on the way to work. I got out of my car at a parking lot.

It is awfully good not to know a hell of a lot, to say what you have to, and leave, your hands in your pockets, whistling, maybe skipping, knowing just one tree for weeks now, as you might have known a new son, and headed for a pink morning.

And so I am content walking in my body to my new job downtown. Once in my life I would have married in a second. I would have married any girl I didn't even know that smiled at me. Once in my life I would have utterly walked out of my small and trembling body and left it behind like a cicada shell or a snakeskin. Yes, I was ready once to inhabit a new body, one gentle yet strong, one whose smile came easily, one with a kinder face than mine.

But now I am content. It is a joy for me to walk into a coffee shop across the street and tell the owner how much I like his *café au lait*, how I am addicted to it, how I'll tell all my friends where I got it and how easy it was to get.

Yet yesterday I worried about how hard a man I really must be. Walking from where I park my car to the medical school, on a busy street (the paint on the buildings beginning to peel), I saw a man pass me and backtrack. He was wearing a tattered shirt and tattered pants that clashed, his face was wrinkled, his forehead stitched like a baseball with specks of blood all over. And he was kind, waving to me, saying: mister, could I ask you something?

Mary Lamont, I have been approached by men like this who wanted money, who said: Hey, mister, I just got off a freight train from Jackson, Mississippi, and I'm kinda down on my luck, could you spare some small change? As a child I gave these men the money they asked for. But when I gave Steve Smith the thousand dollars I worked the whole summer for, to keep his sinking ship of a butcher shop from sinking, and he never gave it back, I cursed the one who breathed life into the lips of beggars. As with a lover I began to fall into the easy traps of "nevers" and "forevers."

At first I thought when I saw this tattered man asking for help: no, I will not give any of my money away, and I'll say: sorry, I really don't have time to talk now. But I gave him a chance to speak. "Excuse me," he said. I recognized the accent. Georgia someplace. "I just got out of the hospital. I was beat up. My wife left me for good, but she gave me this here parking ticket to find my car in a lot." I looked at the stub. Apparently she had parked the car in some lot before she left him lying stitched and broken in the hospital. Poor bastard. He didn't even know where his car was. The stub didn't have an address, just a number. I didn't know how to help him. Like a baffled mechanic, I said "sorry" and walked on into a morning of gray clouds, pink at the edges.

I have always liked fighter jets. So has Raindrinker. Several times in the past months we reminisced about how, as young boys, we glued together plastic pieces of a model airplane to make a small replica that we could either put on a shelf to show our creativity to any kid visiting our room, or we could hold the jet in the air, moving it as if it were flying, and make jet engine sounds with our voices. Sometimes he and I in our separate childhoods would pretend to fly as pilots in two model jets, one in each hand, making gun noises with our breath to simulate an aerial dogfight, as in some war.

This morning I read in the Sunday papers that the Blue Angel naval jets are going to perform their aerobatics this afternoon at Alvin Calendar Naval Air Station in Belle

Chasse, a ways south of New Orleans. The best thing: admission to see the show is free. Raindrinker is glad to come along with me in my old VW. The six jets do amazing precision flight maneuvers like flocks of pigeons in their tight formations circling Jackson Square.

Getting out of the car, we see a red stray cat that looks plump enough to be pregnant with kittens. She comes to us to be petted, and then off she goes toward the crowd, meowing.

The parking lots are full as people by the hundred, dressed in summer attire lounge in lawn chairs they brought along. (It is an unseasonably warm day.) Too, some grandstands have been set up for those who want to sit higher off the ground. An announcer is dressed in full dress uniform. He talks over the PA system, introducing the pilots and their planes as they all do four-point barrel rolls only a few feet above the runway. The announcer says, "Folks, we call this part of the show 'Laissez les bon temps rouler — let the good times roll.' " Everyone applauds, especially all the Cajuns in the crowd.

There is a short lull in the program as the jets, airborne now, get ready for their next stunt. Mr. R. D. says he has to tell me a joke. "Now?" I ask, "I wanna watch the jets."

"It's a quick joke."

"OK, Johnny Carson, go ahead, but I guess you know there are thousands of unemployed comedians out there, and you'll fit right in."

But I underestimate the power of the joke, which R. D. delivers in his best East Texas accent. "OK, ole gal lives out in the country calls the fire department. 'Mah house is on fire! Mah house is on fire!' 'Yes ma'am, *how* do we get there?' 'Ain't you boys still drivin' 'at same red truck?' " Well, it hits me so hard I'm bent over in laughter.

"Raindrinker," and I'm still in hysterics, "couldn't you have told me this *before* we got to the airshow?"

By this time the announcer is ready to speak again. "Here they go," he says in an enthusiastic voice. The six jets, formed in the shape of an arrowhead climb high at amazing speeds, and all release red, white, and blue smoke at the same time, which honors the country in the same way rifles cracked to a 21-gun salute to honor the fallen President Kennedy at Arlington National Cemetery in 1963.

Somehow, however, Raindrinker begins to feel nauseous. He goes behind a tree to take care of his problem, which I can hear from where I stand.

"You OK?" I ask as he returns.

"Not so good," he says. "Could you drive me back to the French Quarter? Judy will give me something for my stomach and put me to bed."

"Sure, guy, still, I know you wouldn't have missed this for the world."

6.

Mary, I might as well tell you. And you, too, Steve, listen up, you might learn something. You'll flinch, I know. Another job. Oh, Mary, we would have never made it together anyway. People love me in interviews! They all want to hire me!

Let me tell you my first observation about the medical school. Some people in America bad-mouth doctors, even sue: "Too expensive," or "My son only got worse." But most people simply love to mention doctors' names. "Oh, do you know that wonderful neurologist on St. Charles Avenue?" Or: "I saw that cute cardiologist at a party." And most often: "That great pediatrician treated my kid.

I recommend him highly." Surgeons and pathologists I find mentioned least. Maybe because they delve into that hidden, sacred world no one is supposed to see: the inner dark of one's body.

And if you're a doctor people will think you know all the doctors, asking you if you know *their* doctor.

Dr. Harry Levine, a geneticist with impressive accomplishments in his field, has worked together with the same secretary for years now, he with the scar on his upper lip and she with the beautiful auburn hair. The week before the Easter holidays she probably didn't really feel like talking, but asked anyway.

"Harry, does your wife work?

"Why?"

"Just curious."

"Nope."

"Why not?"

"Cause she married a nice guy like me." He smiled.

"You know," she laughed between words, "that's what I should have asked my husband before we got married: Will I have to work? Instead I said silly things like: do you love me?" "My husband's a nice guy, too," she added, "but poor."

I had just made coffee. "Don't expect any work out of me," I tell Dr. Levine. "I was hired for my physique." If you look at him closely, you'll see him walk around with his lips pressed lightly and kind of drawn in. I guess it means modesty.

The secretary asks me to Xerox a letter. "Me? I'm new here. Sorry," I say, so she shows me how to use the thing.

Dr. Levine often lets me take trips, which breaks the monotony of the office. In a bar in Shreveport, seven hours by car from New Orleans. The five o'clock sun pouring in a glass door. You remove your sun glasses so swiftly, with such professionalism, that I like it. I am a sucker for girls who walk in bars late afternoons. But you are with someone, so I figure I haven't got a chance to get acquainted.

My trip here from New Orleans was pretty uneventful. I drove up here to do family histories on parents whose children had inherited the disease phenylketonuria, or PKU, in which phenylalanine is not converted in the brain in the normal metabolic sequence to tyrosine. Babies are all tested after birth in the hospital, and if they have the disease they are put on a diet without phenylalanine so that they don't become mentally retarded. In the normal population the incidence of the disease is about one in twenty thousand newborns. But in Cajun Louisiana it is about one in three thousand. It takes two parents to carry the bad gene, and my boss sends me all around Louisiana to make a chart with all the family members, going back four or five generations. We find, in lots of these consanguineous families, second or third cousins have married unknowingly. We use the data, which I obtain, in genetic counseling to tell prospective parents their chance of having a child with the disease. As I said, this is especially true in Southwestern Louisiana in Cajun families. Let's get one thing straight. I'm a Cajun, and I hate people who call Cajuns "Coon Asses." It's nothin' else but pejorative.

The drive was hectic. The roads north from Baton Rouge to Shreveport were all two lanes and their condition was bad as the roads in nineteenth-century Mother Russia.

You have to remember the roads tend here to sink and get full of potholes in a state that is mostly warm pudding.

In Bunkie I stopped for gas, and this one man with a car

having a Colorado license plate was asking a truck driver if he could have some stalks of sugar cane to take back to Colorado. Sugar cane bits and bits of cotton littered the sides of the highway north of Bunkie. Near Natchitoches the cotton fields lining the road still had little pieces of cotton left on the plant.

The day was sunny. No clouds. I wasn't willing to pay the exorbitant rates most of the chain motels charge, so I looked around. I asked this one kind fellow if he knew of any cheap motels with a bed for one. He gave me directions to this one place called Aunt Emma's. (Someone once told me never to eat at any place called Mom's.) It was pretty run down, but cheap: all I really needed. It turns out there's a fried chicken place next door that has a drive-up window to take your orders, if you want to stay in your car. All I kept hearing the whole afternoon, then later at night from my room was: "May I take your order?" And loud too.

So this is Shreveport. Several times I have thought about calling Sue Ellen Fruchtbaum, but I can't. I was supposed to marry her at one time. Three years ago she drove down to New Orleans after I said yes. But as the days went by with us looking for an apartment, it became apparent she was quite schizophrenic. And I mean I just couldn't handle her mood swings. So I told her I couldn't marry her, and that wasn't necessarily because she was badly overweight. She got pissed off, saying she drove all the way down and everything. So, in short, even after three years she just might not want to talk to me. I forget how we met, but once in a bar she kept bitching at me, and my poet friend, drinking with us, said: "Why the hell don't you leave Kent alone?" Then she dumped her mixed drink into his lap. We were all speechless.

Here at the motel at night I hear the plumbing rattle every time someone turns on the water. Mop handles fall, doors slam, traffic roars. It's impossible to get any sleep in a motel next to a major highway.

7.

As I said once before, I'm not a real talker when it comes to sitting around the kitchen table. But that's only with *my* family. With strangers it's different. When I take family histories of people around Louisiana I've never met before, we always sit around the kitchen table. Dr. Levine has been with me on several occasions and has complimented me on my ability to get information from people. All, of course, done with a certain amount of professionalism.

As a boy I didn't like to do jobs for my family. Instead I'd go down the block to Bobby Sanchez's house and help his mother make tea, though my mother said his mother had TB or something, she heard, and I shouldn't drink out of her glasses. Or I'd help Mr. Sanchez fix his car. It's terrible, but I used to like to be around everybody else's mothers and fathers.

I'm not gonna talk much more about my sister. Tonight she took off the old wax on the kitchen floor and put down new wax. She watches TV, goes to work and is never late, carries her umbrella when the weatherman predicts rain, is a secretary, has one boyfriend, laughs at jokes but doesn't understand most of them, has given up all hope of becoming an airline stewardess, sometimes pouts, is embarrassed listening to her own voice on a tape recorder, is, in short, pretty boring.

Last year she gathered up all the photographs of our

family, those scattered in different drawers, and put them in albums. She also has a high school scrapbook which she works on diligently. Twenty now, she rarely raises her voice above a monotone.

(She can get angry however.)

There is a picture in the album I just saw after many years. There are two sixth graders in suits accepting awards from the grammar school principal. I'm one, and the other is a boy named Dante J. O'Malley. I saw him last in high school more than ten years ago, and just for the hell of it I look up his name in the New Orleans phone book and find a D. J. O'Malley. I don't think he ever liked the name "Dante." This is funny because I'm not listed in the phone book, and if some old friend ever wanted to look me up, they'd never find me. Still, there are advantages living where you grew up.

Saturday I call him. Wife answers. He's taking a nap, could he call me back? That midnight I awaken to the phone, and it's him. Turns out he works near the medical school where I work. We arrange to have lunch.

Monday morning I typed and filed. I don't usually do that, but it had to be done. I put my hands behind my head, leaned back, stretched. My throat made a noise. Often, in the middle of work, I'd practice what I'd say on the Dick Cavett Show in an interview. In answer to a question about writers, I'd say: you don't have to be crazy to be a writer, but it helps. Then the audience would laugh and applaud. I practice impersonations in front of my thought piano for half an hour. Maybe this job is not for me. If I were the editor of a local literary magazine, I'd call it *Riverground, Riverearth,* or *Riverlands,* our being next door to the Mississippi River and all. Just a thought.

I left for lunch early and walked over to Room 100 in

Building A where the social workers keep themselves. I recognized Dante there among his colleagues, even after more than ten years. Only now he had a moustache, and his hair was longer.

"Hi, Dante."

"Hey, stranger," he said in a quiet voice. "What's it been, more than ten years?"

He introduced me to his co-workers as a high school buddy, then we went to a small lunch room down the hall.

He said, "You put on some weight, huh?" He leaned back on the chair, propping his feet on the table. Even in grammar school he was always one to relax. He played baseball in high school. Had a throwing arm that was both strong and accurate. His little finger was crooked where a ball hit it, snapping it out of joint. Back then, frightened, he just couldn't pop his finger back in place, so I did it for him. We were on the same team that day. We lost.

At the Hospital of New Orleans local folks come as well as poor people from around the state. For most, to talk is enough. Take this one lady, who comes in the room looking for Dante for the third time in an hour, and tells him about how the doctor didn't give her the right medicine cause her stomach still hurts. This black woman must be sixty. Dante is patient. He tells her where she might go to see the doctor she needs. After fifteen minutes talking, she leaves. Dante finally kept saying: "OK, Mrs. Fitzgerald, OK, OK, OK...."

"Dante, do you remember 1964? Well, in the summer I was still sad over President Kennedy's death. I was fifteen. One day, riding the bus home I remembered when I was eight. Those days we had money. In my father's pocketbook lying on the dresser as he slept in the afternoon, I counted out the crisp ones, old fives, new tens, a few twenties. Father would say: people who write on money should be put away. Mother would agree. I'd disagree silently. Do what the hell you want as long as you don't hurt anyone. Back then, even the big letters on the billboards looked blurry to me. They had me fitted with black-rimmed glasses. I'd sit in the hot Plymouth while the grown-ups went shopping. They said I touched too much. I swore, if they didn't bring me back somethin', anything, I'd cry for a long time, and they'd be sorrier than a woman who lost two husbands."

"I remember 1964. Remember? My father died in a fire." Silence.

"You married?"

"Yep. Two kids."

"I'm single but looking. I've had some pretty bad luck with women, but I rethought the whole situation. At first I believed it was me who was being rejected by women my age. But then it occurred to me that maybe I was getting all the losers, who made it into their late twenties and early thirties alive, but crazy."

"A good way to look at it. Hell, there are plenty of 'em out there."

"Dante, remember a guy named Frisoli?"

"Yeah, he was sort of different."

"He was twelve years old when his heart made its last fist. There were two cowlicks at the crown of Frisoli's blond head that ran into each other like two pinwheels twirling in the opposite direction. His teeth were shades of green, and the front tooth was chipped at an angle. His body was somewhat dwarfed, his fingers were stubby, and his nails were bitten to the flesh. Had a face full of freckles and a pug, almost flattened nose.

At least three times a day Frisoli stopped anything he

was doing to perform a ritual for a friend whose name was too sacred for him to mention. He would extend his left foot and point to it with his right forefinger. He'd squint one eye, as if to aim, and twirl endless, effortless circles. Endless zeroes toward the dust on the top of his shoe."

"Why did you recall Frisoli?"

"I dreamt about both of you last night. He was pumping gasoline to cars for free, and you were his manager, and you just kept beating him on the head, as if you were trying to pound him into the ground. The poor little guy. Not only crazy, but dead at twelve."

We decided to drive over to a small hamburger place near the hospital. The hamburgers were good because they were thick, juicy, and cheap. Dante turned out to be one of those people who liked to look around when they drive and say, "Hey looka that," his eyes not on the road. And that bothered me.

This was one of the older sections of town. The old, huge oaks were many, lining the streets. The cemeteries had dates going back to the mid-eighteenth century, and unused, rusted railroad tracks must have been there a long time.

From the outside looking in, I could see the same little retarded-looking boy with a puffy, red face, who I'd seen for so long around the hospital. And there, too, was the shirtless black dude, who walked the streets every day, bare-footed and with his trousers rolled up to his knees. He had a limp to his walk, as though one leg were shorter than the other. He drooled and passed the back of his hand across his lips. Then he winked at us as we opened the door.

Dante and I sat and talked of the physics experiments that never worked, of the dumpy physics teacher himself, who wore a greenish toupee and used to say every morning to the dumb ones who couldn't answer his questions: "Any common man can read the newspaper, but it takes no common man to estudy physics (fee-sicks). You must estudy, boys and girls." We being seniors in high school. We remembered the names of the two caught undressed and making love (they probably didn't get very far) on the third floor staircase by an early janitor. We remembered how both of us were young-looking, thin-wristed, and how we never took girls seriously. And we remembered the death of a popular football player one August before school started, in a fiery car crash in 1965.

The little red-faced boy was pounding on his hamburger, looking around toward the ceiling and contorting his neck. It all seemed great fun to him.

"Anyone we knew left in our old neighborhood just off the eastbound highway?" Dante asked.

"No, we're still there, but it's sad, sad, everyone getting affluent and moving away from the blacks to new subdivisions."

The real estate agents in the neighborhood were unscrupulous people. They'd mail you these post cards with nothing but "Another one moved in your neighborhood. If you think of selling, see us first." The whole thought of it infuriated me. In the old days, late fifties and early sixties, Dante and I lived on either side of a poor black neighborhood, which was just off the highway heading east towards Mississippi.

As Dante spoke to me, my mind couldn't help drifting in and out, as I thought of that neighborhood, just off the main highway east where I'd lived most of my life.

The highway is U. S. 90. At one point it follows the Mississippi River for a ways. They called it the Old

Spanish Trail once. From California to Florida it unwinds river-like, and never as the crow flies. Hudson oil. Cheap gas. Bulk oil set on racks, near the pumps, in those jars. 1963. The bulk oil is 15 cents per quart. Down the road is competition. Billups. "Fill up with Billups," the signs said. The governor of Louisiana had shares in it. Six men rush out to your car the moment you pull up. You think they're going to change your tires like the pit men at the Indianapolis 500 Speedway. Or you think they'll lift your car to inspect the muffler. They don't. But good service. No green stamps, however, like they give at Esso or Texaco. Instead they give (at Billups) the same kind of prizes as amusement parks, provided that you buy enough gas there. Maybe they'll give out a set of glasses with black quails embossed on them. All for eight gallons or more. It's cheaper if you put it in yourself. Some do. You hear the numbers unwind your life in figures with the ringing of a bell every ten-cent spin. Like a roulette wheel. Or those wire barrels spinning with the ticket — somewhere among the thousands — that you put in to try to win a raffle. Once I won an automatic toaster from a small Negro Catholic church on the highway. It was rebuilt from wood to brick after a tornado, unusual for these parts, wiped out the first building. And the grocery stores. Italian owned and operated. A big sign: "If you can't stop, smile as you go by." And places for hamburgers, Frostops with gigantic root beer mugs spinning faster than it takes a satellite to orbit the earth. Malts whirl in the automatic blender as you would in that machine at the amusement park where the bottom falls out, and you stick to the sides. Malts are up a nickel. French fries to go — they forget to put the packs of ketchup in the take-out bag. The windows in the car are down, and the rain has come. The Hollywood

Palms Motel, whose swimming pool wasn't cleaned until this week when they charge local kids so little money that they don't hop the fence, has the no vacancy sign lit up. Others, less presentable. The Top Motel. A flashing neon toy top six feet tall. And the Horse Carriage Motel. Two plastic life-size horses drawing an original weather-beaten carriage with the fringes on top. Prices down from three-fifty to three dollars a night. No air-conditioning. And a dog kennel with an around-the-clock veterinarian.

Six years ago they widened the highway. From four lanes to six, now with elevated neutral grounds so kids and dogs could cross half-way and not risk getting hit by traffic coming in both directions. Now that the Interstate, that telephone line of highways, is being worked on only a mile away, the old highway entrepreneurs are worried. Motel owners are worried. So are store owners. So are the people at the gas stations who used to give away teddy bears to the kids for eight gallons or more. So are the hamburger places that have been making sure to put in extra ketchup packs in take-out bags. So are the twenty-four-hour-a-day restaurants that used to serve a lot of coffee to truck drivers. Only the bowling alley is not worried so far. Bowling is fashionable. People will drive for miles to bowl. So the bowling alley is an evergreen among flowers that come and go with the season. Many establishments change hands. Not the bowling alley. The same man has held controlling interest since they built it years ago. Along with his lounge, next door, which has dancing girls.

Sometimes the bowling alley's parking lot is so full that someone's car will get stolen. I am fourteen. A friend of mine is stealing a brand new 62 Chevy. Someone must have left his keys in the ignition and the doors unlocked.

Those guys make it so easy. My friend waves at me as he makes the tires squeal out of the parking lot. This is east New Orleans. The cops in Boone, North Carolina finally catch up with him. Ship him home. You'd think his parents would give a damn. They don't.

It had begun to rain. Dante looked at me through the tops of his glasses, while I looked out of the huge glass window, and he said: "Hey man, where are you?"

"Just thinking." Looking out through the rain-battered pane of glass I realized, as when my mother had died, that I was a lapsed Catholic. I wondered if Dante kept up with his religion.

"You still go to church?"

"Yeah, we were married in the Church. My two boys go to Catholic schools now."

I wanted to explain to him how I had not been to church in years, how I was a kind of pantheist, seeing God everywhere, and how I was reading Sartre, who said that existence precedes essence and that essentially there are no excuses and one man was responsible for all men in a philosophical way. But I didn't. It occurred to me that every time I put on a few more pounds, I lost a little bit more religion in its place.

"Dante, you know these girls at work were talking to another girl, about to be married, talking of all their china and silverware they had picked out before their own marriages. And I just kept silent, not knowing what to say. And when I marry I could never be part of the Church ceremony."

What I didn't tell Dante was what was becoming the pure truth for me: that I might never marry and never have children, though I met women from time to time. Perhaps I was a lone sailor cooking in a ship's galley, or even a drifter who went from hotel to hotel, never quite comfortable in any of the beds. Perhaps I was not the family man my mother had so often wished I would be. Although I was dry and inside, it was like the heaviness of the rain laying weights on my shoulders. Mary Lamont, is this your life? Like me, the last good kiss long ago, or like Dante, the burning images in your mind of your children's school pictures neatly in frames by the mirror on your bedroom dresser? Where do the dead go? Why do the clouds burn? Why are the trees so silent in winter?

I continued. "There was this black supervisor I worked for at a coffee plant. I stacked cases of coffee as they came off the assembly line. Never in my life have I admired someone so much as this tiny, thin man, not the Captain of the high school football team, not the President of the student body (also a football player), not even all the National Merit Scholars in high school. From 9 PM till 6 AM he worked at the plant. Then he went home to a wife and six children, slept only two hours that morning. From there he spent the whole day at the university working in an organic chemistry lab. This man told me he would keep at it till he got the Nobel Prize. Did his time in the military, which didn't seem to affect his deep laugh. I wanted so much to take a tape recorder and talk with him to see how in all those years he had gotten his mind set on winning such a prize. Why isn't this my life? Why isn't it yours?" Dante kind of nodded as I went ahead with my tirade.

"Sometimes I envision throwing a great party for all the inhabitants of my city, one even greater than Mardi Gras. And perhaps a few, but even that is good enough, perhaps just a few will meet new people and make new friends."

Dante was nodding his head quite rhythmically, but

that's all. He finished the last of his hamburger and fries. "Say, man, your hamburger's getting cold."

"Oh, yeah." I pushed it away and sipped the last of my beer. Dante stood up, sort of nervous to leave fast. Near the edge of the table by my feet I watched a quick mouse hug close to the wall and disappear into some hole that looked smaller than it was.

8.

I've become a victim of that black hermaphroditic monster again, but I hadn't seen Dante in a week and wanted to call him, to let him know I'd like to visit him and his wife and children. We wound up talking on the phone a long time. I asked him about what all his brothers and sisters were doing. I remembered them from years ago.

Our tenth high school reunion was only the year before. Dante did not go. I asked him why. "Oh, you know," he said. "I'm not much of a socializer." We talked about some of all the people we both knew back then, how the valedictorian had become a fireman, and how the high school newspaper editor had become a prize-winning body builder and weight lifter, in addition to his selling carpets for a living.

"Dante, I remember something you told me back in the fifth grade. I asked you if you wanted to study with me one night, and you told me you'd wait till you got to college to study hard. Those were your exact words twenty years ago." He laughed. He talked very rapidly, said "you know" a lot, and sometimes embarrassedly slurred over a word or two, so I'd have to ask him briefly "What say?" or "What was that?" When he was ten he wanted to be a mechanical engineer. The same at fifteen, eighteen, but at twenty he quit college, managed a hamburger place for two years, went into the Army, fought in Vietnam, then came back, married, and finally got a degree in Social Work.

"You didn't see what I saw on the way to work this morning," I said.

"What was that?"

"I crossed the light and was looking down the block. I saw a woman pushing a man in a wheelchair to the emergency room of the Hospital of New Orleans. She was pushing him against the light and all these goddamn cars were blowing horns. In the middle of the street he fell forward out of his wheelchair, hit the pavement face down, and froze. His wife screamed, and a man nearby ran for a resident doctor in the hospital. It must have taken a goddamn fifteen minutes for the resident to get there, and the whole time cars blocks away were blowing their horns, all of them trying to get to work. I wonder how many knew who was holding up traffic. The wind was blowing hard. It was about 50 degrees, the last cold before spring really set in. The resident walked briskly to the man, yanked his shirt out, put his stethoscope to the man's chest, and asked if anyone could get a sheet. A man in a blue suit grabbed a piece of painters' canvas, the kind they use to catch wet paint falling. It was speckled black with splotches. The resident gently fitted the canvas over and around the body. Horns were blowing everywhere by now. I was sick and disgusted. I raised my fist to all the cars in the world and yelled out: 'You stupid bastards!' I doubt anyone heard me. 'Sorry,' they must have been thinking, 'no time for the dead.' The dead man's wife was hysterical, yelling 'Oh God, he's gone. What am I gonna do without him?!' And the resident, a bald and bearded young man with the stethoscope still pinching at his neck, had his arms around her. I'll never forget it, the ambulance from the hospital blocks away, unable to get through the traffic. And we might have been only fifty feet from the hospital! I got sick and numb and faced across the street. There was a beautiful young girl, maybe seventeen, with a back pack and a tear or two in her eyes.

She must have seen everything. She saw that I saw. She looked Oriental. Dante, for the first time in my life I ran up to a stranger — teary-eyed the both of us — a stranger I had not even said hello to and hugged her like a sister. She was still hugging me even harder when we sort of stumbled into the café of the bus station, the wind blowing strong. I ordered two coffees, and we sat at a small table with Bentwood chairs. We stared into our coffee for a long time, then she lifted her head. 'I no Engleesh speak. I-, I- from just Detroit come.' Outside the pigeons seemed frightened. We finished our coffee, I held her hand, walked her outside, and gave her to this morning of all those alive and all those not."

"You feel OK now?"

"Yeah, but the whole morning at work I never said a word to anyone."

Dante seemed moved by my story, though not deeply saddened, and I didn't expect him to be. Instead he told me another story he saw years before from his window at the Social Work office. Must have been fifty people standing in line to be treated at the clinic. An old man in line slumped over and a new nurse called the intern. The old man still had the nitroglycerin pill in his hand, so the intern knew. He took a scalpel and slit open the man's chest. Grabbed his heart and started massaging it. Then

Dante looked for the crowd. They had all vanished! Not then, but now telling me this, he laughs. It's sad, sad.

Chapter Six

⚜

1.

Saturday. This morning my father was feeling pretty bad. He needed gas in his car to go to work Monday morning, so I offered to drive it to the station and fill it up, which I did. Lately I've been learning how to sit more comfortably at the kitchen table on the weekend and talk to my father and sister. This morning I spent fifteen minutes talking to my father about the good and bad points of buying a new car, which he couldn't afford now, but if he saved, he could afford in six months. His salary was not bad, but now that Mother was gone, he had to pay more income tax. The week after my mother died, we cleared out the closet of her dresses, hats, and shoes, and gave them away to neighbors, especially Mrs. Wilson next door, a black woman who was about Mother's size. Then father moved his clothes into her closet. How long after death do most people take to replace the dead with the living? I wonder.

Even after her death the doctor bills arrive in my mother's name. There ought to be some way to make the names of the dead sacred only to their tombstones.

Today's mail: one letter, returned by the mailman, which I wrote to a girl in Florida, having learned now that long distance relationships are tricky business and fail more often than not. Her letter was returned because no one by her name was living at that address. How could that have happened? When I drove alone to Florida and met her on the beach, she seemed settled down to her life in Holmes Beach. We corresponded for a month. She must have left on a whim.

Also: one letter, Xeroxed, asking me to vote for a man who is running for assessor, and is taking a stand on low property taxes. Why ask me? I don't own property. Finally, a letter, Xeroxed, asking me to contribute to Tulane University. Did they expect me to succeed by the time I was twenty-nine?

It is raining out. I sit at my desk and scribble thoughts. One of the great acts of creativity is this: to read someone else's work, then perhaps write your own better work, but in a mysterious collaboration of each other's terms. Or: the poet has as much control over changing his voice as he does his own accent. But who would believe it?

And Goethe, speaking through God, said in *Faust*: "*Es irrt der Mensch, solang er strebt*." Even though we strive, we still run a good chance of failure, of going wrong. That's the sad story. But when we strive we stay one step ahead of ourselves, and the stuff of our undoing remains behind us. This is *Werden*. This is becoming the person we will be when the moments are over.

It might all just be unprovable. You see, I don't know: no audience to try it out on. Now if I got on stage with my impersonations of Howard No Sell, John Wayne, and Groucho Marx, now *there* would be something I'd get a response to.

Howard No Sell: Hello folks, this is Howard No *Sell*, who left a dull life practicing law to become what he is today: an obsessive-compulsive, egocentric announcer. And if you're wondering how I got this black eye I'm wearing, it was cause a fighter friend of mine, Ali, knocked me out for talking this way.

John Wayne (as football coach during the Second World War): well, boys, get out there and knock 'em dead. If ya lose this game, I'll call the President and ask him to let ya play John Wayne overseas.

Groucho Marx: Oh, Margaret, my love, let's get married tonight. I can see it all now. Our little cottage in the woods. You standing by the front gate, and me coming home from woik. (Pause.) On second thought, me standing by the front gate, and you coming home from woik.

Oh, Groucho, who lived from 1890 to 1977, if I were an actor by trade I'd sing you this song of praise. You impressed me so much I had to invent you for the women students of Holy Angels School on St. Claude Avenue in 1974. I became you. I put on grease paint for a black moustache, for black eyebrows. I bought the biggest cigar in town. I got a frock, swallow-tailed coat from the Volunteers of America. Shrewd, lovable man, it took me a long time, but finally our voices matched. Your voice was so gentle in its deep tones even insults sounded good, even the morning would have listened to you.

Sunday. At the street corner across from the medical school I stopped to watch a family pitching pennies at the brick wall of an abandoned drug store. Know how it works? The closest penny to the wall wins. Stand up a penny against the wall and that's the closest you can get. "Wanna play?" the mother asked me. "No, sorry. It looks like fun, but I have to get to work."   As I walked across the street, I could hear them still laughing and talking with excited voices.

I worked all afternoon. At the door to my office I found I had forgotten my keys. I said "shit," but then thought about the security guard. He had a master key, and that saved me from driving all the way back home to get my own keys. I came home, finally, at 7 PM, dead tired. My sister and father were watching a movie on TV. I went to the kitchen and ate some peach cobbler. It was all I could find. I didn't want to disturb them in the middle of a movie, so I went to my room.

I kicked off my shoes, fell into bed, clothes and all, and pulled the covers which weren't fixed right. Took off my glasses. Layed them on their sides on the night table. I set the alarm. Passed two fingers of the same hand over my eyes and pressed. Let go.

Saw light behind my eyelids.

In a deep sleep I felt someone waking me. I could barely open my eyes, but the clock said almost midnight. For a split second I was afraid in my dreams. I was startled.

"Did you eat my whole pan of peach cobbler?" I heard my sister say.

"What?" I could barely see. I made out the shape and face of my sister.

"The whole pan of peach cobbler I baked tonight is gone!"

"Say, look," I mumbled, shedding my eyes from the light with my forearm, "it was all I could find."

"Goddamn it, no wonder you're so fat."

"Say, look, would you give me a break?"

"If you eat any more in this house, I'm gonna ask Daddy to raise your rent."

I couldn't get over how she was acting. I mean the

whole thing was no big deal. I worked hard that afternoon, and a *Sunday* of all afternoons, and here she was crawling all over me.

"Say, what the hell's going on with you, anyway? You've never been like this before."

"I'm gonna have him raise your rent. That's what I'm gonna do. And from now on you don't get to eat anything I bake." And she marched out of the room, slamming my door. What do you say to a woman like that? And the daughter of a negotiator! My sister always used to be the little diplomat of the family. Menstrual period, I thought, though not in those words. I was so tired. I sat up in bed, barely able to stay awake. I did the best thinking I could do for about ten minutes. Then I decided I was the one all wrong and would apologize to her. I just couldn't wait till the next morning, even though my eyes told me different. Hell, if I went to sleep now, she was liable to club me to death in my sleep or somethin'. No, I had to settle this thing. She was a sucker for sweet talk.

When I got to the kitchen, I was still in my underwear. Hardly anyone comes to visit us, so I usually don't think twice about running around in my underwear. She was scrubbing the sink with harder strokes than usual. I pulled out a five dollar bill from the black wallet I brought along, the misshapen one my mother had given me five years before on my birthday.

"Here," I held my hand out with the bill.

"I don't want money. It's the principle."

"You know you're harder to bargain with than a needle and thread."

"So?"

"You know you're pretty cute. Won't you give me a smile at least?" Silence. "Pretty please, you cutie."

She turned to me face to face real quick, smiled a quick smile, and faced back to the sink.

"Then you're not angry any more?"

"Oh, I don't know."

I took that as a positive sign. I had the feeling my sister just broke up with her boyfriend. I walked away, the bitten nails of my hands in my underwear like fish.

On Wednesday I awoke restlessly at 4 AM, the time my father usually gets up. In the ten minutes I just lay there, I thought of three questions. The world is so full of people, why isn't it so full of cemeteries? How many places on earth are there where no foot has ever left a track? And: how many times a day has the tired waitress, snatching at her hair, gone back and forth for only coffee, again and again?

Spring, summer, and autumn seemed to fly by while I worked for Dr. Levine at the medical school. It was already November, election time in Louisiana.

To my father in the past few days I have only said hello in the morning, when he leaves for work, and a hi when we each come home from work in the afternoon, almost at the same time. We eat separately. He doesn't eat much, a frozen waffle or two for supper. I have been eating out lately. This morning just a few words brought us together.

"Well, looks like we'll have a new governor by next weekend," he said, and I could sense he was willing to talk about his favorite subject: politics. "You know," he continued, "you really ought to read T. Harry Williams' biography of Huey Long. I think you'd appreciate it." Politics was not my favorite subject, but I just felt in the mood to learn something. And I asked him a lot of questions about Long, like an interviewer. A whole hour! And my father remembered nearly all of what he read and how he grew up during the rise and fall of Huey Long. I won't go into specifics cause it's all pretty local. I've not figured out whether someone from New York, or California, or even Texas next door would be willing to talk about Huey Long. It might just bore them.

But you know what will happen in Louisiana? Just this: A politician, K., a candidate for governor, gets appendicitis and pneumonia a week before the election. It is a cold November. On TV and on radio his opponent attacks him for his voting record in the legislature. To newsmen K. says, from his hospital bed and through a spokesman, that he doesn't feel well enough to answer his opponent's allegations, but will very soon now. For a week the opponent continues to lash out at K. And K., still sick, wins the election by 3 AM Sunday morning, November the Ninth.

2.

The washing machine is making more noise than usual: something is loose. I have that old fear in my bones that my wallet is going to suffer because my father will make me pay half the bill.

That's not so bad really when I think that my sister saved the life of my favorite house plant. It was so sad that all the healthy leaves began drooping over the side of the flower pot. My sister put four Midols in the soil and watered it. The next day the leaves were perky as an American flag in a good wind.

"How did you do it?" I asked her.

"Don't know," she said, "but I'm pretty proud of myself."

"Ever thought about being a plant caretaker?"

"No, but I am now. Mother loved that plant."

Mother. I was just about to cry. But I didn't. A flash went through my head. I am fourteen, in the kitchen with my mother.

"And what are *you* snooping around for?" she asks.

"Something to eat."

"I thought so, Fatso. And why, sir, did you make a scene yesterday taking your sister's bicycle away from her, and riding it down the street standing on the seat on one leg?"

"I told you, Mother, I don't wanna sit in the audience with a passive consciousness. I wanna be on stage."

But you see how it turned out? In this month of the anniversary of my birth, I don't want to be a politician. Bless them. They need blessings. Nor a journalist. Bless them. I don't want to be a policeman or a fireman. Bless them. Not a sports announcer who must sound like every other sports announcer. Bless them. Maybe an actor, maybe a teacher (what's the difference?). Maybe a CEO so I can go to expensive parties in expensive clothes. Almost certainly a doctor. "Oh, what will I be?" sighed the mother, and the father said, "you have been a mother," and they slept dreamlessly the whole night.

But if I'm gonna be a doctor, I'll have to stop certain bad habits. It's funny how people can squander money. Booze. Casinos. Horses. I call, long distance. Tonight I called six girls long distance. One in each place: Baton Rouge, Austin, New York City, San Francisco, Tampa, and Fayetteville, Arkansas. If this keeps up I'll have to eat more chicken soup from a can.

First the washer, now the heater needs to be repaired. My father will make me pay half the bill. I know.

3.

I lost my temper twice today, which happens occasionally. I am not mechanically inclined, or so I tell myself. This morning I tried to put in a new headlight on my car. The old bulb burned out. There were three screws to put in, and this one screw fit in a hard-to-get-at place. I really needed four hands for the whole damned thing. The screw refused to go in. Maybe cursing helped. It finally went in.

All day it has rained. I've been cursing the rain. But my patience showed up later at Dante's. I went over for supper. When I got there, Karen, their two-year-old, was painting the walls with apple juice. She would get the apple juice on the walls by pressing against the nipple of her bottle. Neither Dante nor his wife seemed to mind.

Karen brought me her jack-in-the-box. I turned the crank, and it played a lovely tune, but at the end of the tune Jack would not pop out. I asked Dante for a screwdriver and took it apart. The mechanism looked pretty complicated with little toothed wheels and rubber bands everywhere. I can't say how I fixed it in an hour. Proud of myself, I just pressed and pulled logically at the mysterious inner workings, screwed the top on, and it worked.

Dante's wife walked in with her recent oil painting of a church near a bayou with an oak tree to the far side of the picture. I studied it awhile.

"I like it," I said. "But there's one small flaw."

"What's that?" she asked politely.

"See the live oak, how you've got all brown and green

in it? Well, if you look at a live oak at the same distance as your painter's eye looked at it, you'll find that you can see patches of sky between the leaves and branches."

"You know, you're right," she said. "A good observation."

"I still think it looks good," I said. "Some awfully good poets have gotten their facts wrong in a poem, but that doesn't make the poem any less beautiful."

Karen was tugging at my pants leg. She wanted to show me how she could make Jack jump out of his box. I watched her turn the crank. She instinctively knew where the music ended and Jack popped out. She was pretty clever handing me the box so Jack would scare me. I pretended not to know. When Jack exploded from inside, I made my whole body twitch and tremble as if lightning had struck me. Karen laughed all the way to the supper table.

As I walked to the kitchen their youngest ran up to my leg and said, "Hide me, hide me." His mother had been chasing him all over the house, trying to put a T-shirt over him.

"What's the problem?" I asked Dante.

"Jerry thinks that when we put his T-shirt over him, he'll smother to death."

Good instincts, I thought. "I see," I said. I didn't know what to say. I guess if the kid had these fears, maybe the best thing would be to make him wear shirts that buttoned up the front.

Let's face it, it's good to go to other people's houses for supper. When you're on your own, you just open a can of this and a can of that, throw a piece of meat in the frying pan, and that's your meal. Tonight I was having home-baked lasagna and after it home-made ice cream.

Then Dante gave me a cigar to smoke and a small glass of apricot brandy. I had not smoked a fine cigar in years. Somehow, as a gift, it was better than if I had bought it myself.

4.

I'm closer to trees than to grass, closer to grass than to mud. Ask the owl: it knows how I feel, a slow mouse in its beak.

I swear I don't even know what month it is, they've gone by so fast. Oh yes, it's March 1st, my father's birthday. All he expects is we wish him a happy birthday. He doesn't expect presents. My father is not a spender. He needs a new car. Today I asked him when he would get one. "Oh," he sighed. "I'm in no hurry." It's like these people who called up today asking if they could inspect our house to see if there were places burglars could easily break into. I heard him on the phone: "You tryin' to sell me somethin'?" he asked. "Well I hate to sound rude, but I'm tired of people calling me up to sell me somethin'. It's an invasion of privacy."

"I'm not worried about burglars," he told me. "There's nothing worth stealing in this house except a television that doesn't work half the time anyway. They can have it." My father's voice has been clear and calm all this time. He's a negotiator, and he knows how to deal with people so shrewdly he doesn't make them angry.

He rarely even makes me angry anymore. "I don't want to hurt your feelings or anything, but you know you've been making an awful lot of expensive phone calls long distance lately. Of course, you're usually paying for them, but I'd bet you'd feel a hell of a lot better writing letters

instead. So what are you going to do about your problem?"
"I dunno. It's as though I were throwing my money away on the horses, I guess. Maybe I should disconnect the phone."

"No, I don't think that's the solution. Whenever you get the urge to call long distance, sit down with a pencil and paper and write your heart out. You'll have to find some constructive way to change your behavior."

"Yes, you're right," I said.

I remember bringing both my socks with me to the chair to put on my shoes. Where the hell is the second sock? For fifteen minutes I looked all over my room for the second sock, trying to retrace my steps. Well, I'll be. I'd put it on my shoulder somehow. In the end it's fifteen minutes of cursing that matters.

Chapter Seven

1.

Granted that Mr. Raindrinker folds balloons when he wants to. But he's a moody kind of guy at times. And at those times he doesn't even feel like having anything to do with balloons or being a clown. Like me, sometimes he likes disguises, sometimes not. What eccentric can I talk to? I suppose I could talk to myself. No. I am not good at supplying the other part of the conversation by myself. Today I met Mr. Raindrinker in my personal suite (Ha!), which is a convention room in a fancy hotel. He is a salesman for a pharmaceutical company which tries to get pediatricians to recommend their product to young mothers. Mr. Raindrinker reassures me that breast-feeding is not always practical or possible, so his artificial formula, high in iron, comes closest to natural mothers' milk.

Mr. Raindrinker and I are attending a seminar here in my hotel lobby, a seminar for geneticists, about which we know nothing. The topic is mucopolysaccharidosis and glycogen storage disease. The lecturer is a PhD-MD who speaks with an accent, tells dirty jokes at parties, and has a great personality. But Mr. Raindrinker and I understand none of the technical aspects, even when members of the audience, learned men, start shouting at one another. We are just here at the bar drinking scotch-and- sodas, which he always pays for.

The lecturer, a Middle-Easterner, is showing slides as he explains how his patient, a sad-looking two-year-old expired recently because—and I'm putting the reason in my own words—medical science still doesn't know everything. Nor is there a carrier detection test for this disease, which, if there were one, would let prospective parents in affected families know if they will have an abnormal child. Yet this is all I understand.

Next the moderator gets up to the microphone and says next year the meeting will be in Memphis, Tennessee instead of Kent Soileau's personal suite. Everyone is nicely dressed. On my hot-table there are morsels of fried chicken without the bone, Swedish meatballs, and quiche. The bartender is a woman, and every time I look up from my conversation with Mr. Raindrinker, she is staring at me. I notice one man with a cleft lip beneath a moustache and one lady with a deformed hand, well concealed.

Mr. Raindrinker is nearly drunk now, though he says he must return to his wife who is in labor at the hospital. "Even if I sell artificial baby formulas," he reassures me, touching my sleeve lightly, "my kid will definitely be breast-fed."

No one is supposed to know this: one of the geneticists here is about to be fired. She apparently has a personality clash with her boss. I know her casually. Have asked her three times to go to bed with me. No luck.

"Good-bye, Mr. Raindrinker," I say, "I hope your wife doesn't need an episiotomy."

✳

My sister, Beth, has gone away to college in another town, my brother David hardly ever visits me, and my father has recently lapsed into an aesthetic silence. So I need Mr. Raindrinker to tell my stories to, to hold conversations with, and, generally, to lead me into worlds of newer and better things. He is really my invisible friend, like Harvey the six-foot rabbit. I've lost track of most of the people I mentioned earlier: Cap'n Peck, Cap'n Miller, the whole group at River Parish Ship Service. I've even come to almost forget, after seven years, Steve Smith and Mary Lamont. I kiss the money good-bye. And love? Oh well, what is love anyway? Dante I hardly ever see. He has his family to worry about. I've lost my job, too, at the medical school. The money from the government grant ran out. So now I'm idly collecting unemployment. What will I do? Why is it that every day I have to plan to have someone or some thing in my life? There is one exception to the people I've lost track of. Even this relationship is bizarrely drawing to a close.

I know the name of the girl who comforted me in the first chapter. Out of anger I won't mention her name. Oh, hell, it's Pam Weiss. I was then about to compare her to Lisawetta in Thomas Mann's *Tonio Kroeger*. However, she is no longer as (what can I say here?) faithful, energetic, and loyal as Lisawetta was.

In short, she's had a sudden change of heart about me, and what came out in the phone conversation was a complicated set of transactions that I still don't understand. I met Pam several years ago. She lived in a house on Banks Street near the state university in Baton Rouge. She was an incredibly thin girl. I liked thin girls best then and still do. Her nose: very Napoleonic. (Once I saw a death mask of Napoleon in the Cabildo in New Orleans.) And what was great was her nose didn't have the flaw in it Napoleon's had. So, besides her nose whose bridge was very nicely high on her forehead, I liked the way she painted her fingernails an incredible shade of brown. And her toenails too. In the summer, when she wore sandals from Mexico with the open end, I could see two nice toes painted that same shade of brown. She would let me come up and pull on her toes. I wouldn't pull too hard. Of course, her sandals were so constructed that I could only grab two of the five. And I wanted them all, but some people are greedy. I suppose that was all nonsense. I really enjoyed gazing up at her brown eyes, the eyes of my mother.

As far as I could tell, she never bought very many new clothes. Either she went to second-hand clothing stores or she just let the years pass and let her clothes grow old. Maybe this was just a fad then of all eighteen-year-old freshmen majoring in the arts. But back then, the first night she invited me over for dinner, she made an exception and was wearing a stunning new dress. I saw how fine it was the minute she unlocked the door. It was blue, low cut so her small breasts peeked out, and it was two inches above the knee. One knee had a small scar on it. It didn't detract, however, from the wholesomeness of her legs at all. When I was eighteen and kissing a woman's leg, a scar would have bothered me. Not then, having come of age. You believe me when I say I did all that at eighteen? I just say that. I was really modest.

Anyway, last night I call up this woman I have the greatest esteem for. "Pam, would you give me a lift downtown? My car's not running."

"Kent, you know I told you my kidneys were giving me trouble, and I couldn't get around much, and here you are asking me for a favor, knowing my condition. You know what you are? You're a taker and not a giver. You know how to manipulate people to get what you want. I think you ought to start helping more people out and asking a little less for yourself. Why don't you call one of your other friends. You seem to call me only when you need to."

"Hey, what the hell, that's not true. All you had to say when I asked for a ride was 'no' and I would have understood." But I was too late. She'd probably hung up before I said any of it. Mr. Raindrinker will pull me through this. He tells me he has contacts with other women even though he's married. It's on to newer and better things.

Mr. Raindrinker told me he once shoplifted at a supermarket. He was in the coffee aisle and couldn't resist putting the package of coffee under his coat. He said when he touched the coffee and thought about stealing it, he felt a tingling in his loins and an act of forbiddance in his mind. He said he felt they owed him the coffee because someone had held him up once with a gun for ten dollars. "An eye for an eye," he said.

Besides, he added, those stores make too much money anyway.

He likes how I say: "It's sad, sad." And now I've got him saying it.

He gets annoyed at people who don't move when the stop light turns green, and he tells me the women he sees without his wife knowing it are still insecure because they still talk about their ex-husbands during their entire evening together.

My father has broken his aesthetic silence this morning, but only to say: "Son, we'll have to make an effort to start cleaning up more around the house. You left your supper dishes for me to wash." Then he went back to working on a one-act play that he has not managed to finish in four years. He perfects and perfects, never finishes. It's funny though about house cleaning. My mother, bless her heart, insisted, when she was alive, that the house be absolutely spotless, which is crazy since we never invited anybody over to see how clean it was.

Mr. Raindrinker tells me he would rather have his solitude than anything else. Understand this: there is nothing funny going on between us. We are mental friends and will keep it that way.

For the past few weeks we have been drinking together, as usual, at the Rusty Nail Bar. Did I already say it was uptown, near the river, just off Carrollton Avenue, a street lined with those great live oaks? I don't wanna have to repeat myself. Tonight Mr. Raindrinker astounded his friends at the bar. He took a beer bottle, turned it upside-down on the top of a five-dollar bill and said he would "give the five dollars to anyone who could remove the bill from under the beer bottle without touching the bottle." Immediately everyone thought of that one old trick where, in the movies, someone yanks the table cloth from under the dishes, leaving the dishes perfectly in place. So one big guy, six-foot-two, 235 pounds, put his two fingers between the bill and yanked. But the bottle tumbled over. Everyone at the bar booed.

"Tell us how, tell us how," everyone shouted. "We give up." Then Mr. Raindrinker, like the magician he was, seized the bill in his left hand, made a fist with his right, pounded on the table top with even strokes and slowly slid the bill from under the bottle, leaving the bottle standing. Mr. Raindrinker's friends all roared in homage.

On the huge mirror behind the bar there was a sign that said: Bartender Wanted For Thurs., Fri., Sat Nites. Apply With Manager. I thought immediately I could use the money, being out of a job. The bartender pointed out to me the manager who was sitting alone at the end of the bar drinking. I walked over to him, Mr. Raindrinker behind me. I introduced myself politely and asked about the job.

"Well, I dunno," he said, not looking at me. "What do you know about bartending?" he asked, looking away. I was beginning to get annoyed. Here was this little five-foot-two-inch manager, practically ignoring me, and completely indifferent to my well-being. I felt safe with Mr. Raindrinker behind me. He was six feet tall and weighed 265 pounds. Then the manager said nothing for a long time, still looking away from me. The little creep had a bulbous nose and a small receded cleft chin. In short, a twerp. I knew of Raindrinker's presence like an intimidator. "Listen, you little pip squeak bastard," I said to the manager, grabbing his shirt at his throat, "I don't like your goddamn attitude. The next time you talk to me you fix your eyes on me and talk as if I meant something as a human being." The little creep was speechless. He gulped down the rest of his bourbon-and-water, said excuse me, and walked out of sight, into the back room.

Mr. Raindrinker unfolded his arms, patted me on the back, and we walked out, content.

My friend predicts that soon there will be no more places to park your car in America. Witness, he says, the cab drivers who park in the middle of the street. He is not trying to cause a panic. It is merely what he calls "Raindrinker's Omen."

Driving around town with me, Mr. R. D. points out

the little things I don't see: the north wind in the street musses the hair. When the light turns green, a crowd is in the middle of the street. The cars accelerate. All the crowd steps back to the neutral grounds, except for one tiny boy who shoots across the street to the other side and almost gets hit. "I'm going to make an observer out of you yet," my friend tells me.

Mr. R. D. says he is a poet, though he has not shown his poems to anyone. He is afraid to. "My poems are love poems," he says, "and they are too personal. I would never want them to be published. There is a poet who has published three books of poems, and she is thirty-one now. Her picture appears on the back of all her books. I am in love with her, yet I am no Rilke, Stevens, or Yeats. I wish there were some way I could write her. They say she lives in the country near Charlottesville, Virginia where she teaches at the university. I am in love with her poems and that picture of her. Soileau, do you think we could start corresponding? Maybe I could write her publisher for her address."

"Mr. Raindrinker, I publish poems, so I know. Everyone I meet I tell I write poetry to says immediately: Oh, I used to write poetry a long time ago. But where is it? I ask you. If it's there, I want to see it. It's not fair to write poetry and hide it from friends for a lifetime. My friend, I like you and don't want to hurt your feelings, but you are what Thomas Mann called a dilettante. Still, Mann was wrong in one sense. Suffering because one is a bourgeois condemned to be an artist doesn't make an artist. Sure, we all die several times in a lifetime, and swallowing a bottle of sleeping pills is tempting. Patience, however, and years of learning to see—which you keep telling me—are what counts. Scientists and artists are not unlike. The scientist calls seeing 'empiricism' while the artist calls it 'art.' They're really the same. And in both scientific research and art, you have to know what not to do, which means you should know everything that's been done. But enough. Did you change jobs again, which is what I'm guilty of too?"

"Yes, I'm afraid so. It seems to me to be what my father told me. He said there are two things a man can't handle: pussy and money."

Something is wrong with him, even with all his wisdom. Lately, like a New England grandmother he replies "that's nice, oh that's nice" to everything I tell him. If I tell him I wrote a poem that pleased me he says "that's nice." If I tell him, Mr. Raindrinker, I've decided to lose weight, and I really mean it this time, he says "that's so nice." How will I break him of his boring replies? It's sad, sad.

I was not surprised that spring, real spring, was so slow in coming. With pain everything slows down. I was barely eking out an existence on the paltry checks I was sent from my unemployment insurance. I was far from starving. Needed clothes and couldn't afford to buy any. And my old car needed repairs badly. The week before a man ran into the back of my VW and messed up the engine. He was a poor black guy without insurance (like me), and it was such a hassle that I decided not to call the cops or make any threats. But as for me, I can talk about whatever you want to hear.

Tell you a story, Mr. Raindrinker? OK. My sister came home from college in Lafayette to spend the weekend. Saturday morning we decided to take all the junk that had been piling up in our back yard to the city dump. It was a pretty day. We rented a pick-up truck with her money. The junk: leaves and branches from back yard trees my father had cut and piled up; an old rusted-out air conditioner; two single-bed mattresses, rotted out; a rusty tricycle that was my sister's fifteen years before; a barbecue pit, rotted through; stones; broken dishes; in short, a graveyard for the excrement of man and nature.

We loaded up the truck in an hour. My father helped me lift the heavy air conditioner up to the very back, so when Beth and I got to the dump, we could just push it off the back without having to lift it. On top of the branches we put the two mattresses and the skeleton of a Christmas tree, months given to decay.

I swear I had no idea of what would happen to us. Anything you do for the first time is pure chance, and anything goes. Not until something sinisterly funny happens, and you feel the adrenalin pulsing hard through your entire body do you sense the nearness to death, the nearness of the body crying out: *let me go, release me* into that kingdom of total freedom, where nothing pulses, where you enter into the vanishing.

And so, as in much of our lives, we felt at one with the cosmos when I eased our loaded-down pick-up on to the interstate and slowly accelerated with the great weight on our backs. We chatted about how much fun her student life was in Lafayette, Louisiana, how spring was finally here, how I went dancing every Thursday night at the Rusty Nail Bar where every Thursday a Cajun band played on into the drunkenness of everyone there. Even shy, non-dancers would get up the nerve and dance after a few drinks, and every week the crowd would get larger and larger. One night the crowd would get so large, it occurred to me, that I would have to do like a character in one of Wolfgang Hildesheimer's stories and use a hammer and a chisel to break my way through one of the walls.

My sister and I were both laughing when I casually glanced in the rear-view mirror. We were doing sixty. I saw the wind gently peel off the Christmas tree from the top of the heap. The mattresses took off too. Oh shit, I thought. We were at the bottom of a high overpass, the worst of all places to be. Cars coming over the top would have no warning of those giant obstructions, the Christmas tree and the mattresses, now lying in the middle of the highway.

It pained me to know I was responsible. And then I heard it: brakes squealing and the dull thuds. I covered my ears. Six times: boom, squeal, boom, squeal, boom, squeal. I stopped the truck. My sister realized what happened. We got out of the truck and saw several cars piled up with their fenders smashed. Thank God it looked like no one was hurt. I remember seeing a tiny dog standing by his master's car wheel start shaking. I was shaking too. I decided to get the hell out of here. "Grab the Christmas tree, Beth. I'll grab the mattresses." We threw the shit back on the pick-up. Then I went as fast as I could to the first exit.

Neither Beth nor I could say anything all the way to the dump. But I bet we were both thinking: what if someone got our license plate number and called the cops. It was a risk we had to take.

My rented truck bounces as Beth and I drive through the deep holes of the dump. Here, at the edge of New Orleans where the woods and the swamplands begin, it is truly a wasteland. In the pink afternoon of last light, the crows cry out to the kingdom of birds and rise by the thousands into one great, dark cloud that moves slowly upwards, as if by wind. This would be the edge of the world if it were flat.

2.

It was Friday night, and it had been a long week. I gave Mr. Raindrinker the night off to spend at home alone. He told me he was trying to write a play. I only half believed him.

My father and I have been pretty close this week. Monday I brought his car and my car to be repaired. Mine had an oil leak somewhere and his had blown a head gasket. Tuesday night I picked up my car, drove it home. I checked the engine. It was still leaking oil. Wednesday I brought it back. It took them till today, Friday, to fix it, and I brought it home only to find it is still leaking oil. What is wrong with mechanics today? Do they know what they are doing? And now, sitting here at the kitchen table with my father, me ready to cook us both some scrambled eggs, he tells me his car runs worse than it did before they fixed it.

"Well, Pa, I am disgusted. I'm ready to push my car off some pier into Lake Pontchartrain."

"Me, too," he said. And we both laughed belly laughs for a long time. Sometimes you just have to laugh at the folly of being human.

We both decided to relax and watch the 6 P. M. local news. The usual. Labor union strikes at an oil refinery. A bank robbery. Political bribes. A local city councilman is resigning to take care of his wife, dying of cancer. The news itself is disheartening. Sometimes they will show a human interest story to let you know everything isn't so bad.

My father sleeps in the room my mother died in. Her bed stays made all the time now. Only his bed stays messed up. When I was twelve, my mother stayed up with me most of the nights of my strange childhood with sickness after sickness. They decided not to sleep together after that, and from then on they slept in different rooms. The night my mother refused to hug me when I cried out in terror of the darkness, I fell asleep to more bad dreams, and, half-asleep, I walked to what I thought was the toilet. It turned out to be my father's bed, an old couch that folded. I pulled down my pajama bottom and pissed on his feet in a dream. He jumped up and shook me awake. "I'm sorry, Dad. Forgive me." To this day he forgives me for pissing on his feet.

I'm thirty now, and my father and I are getting closer and closer. Sometimes I'll see him and say, "How are you feeling?" Tonight he came to me, after years of my going to him, and he asked *me* for advice! What was the best way to get to a mechanic across town? I told him in a gentle voice, then walked him to his bed, the bed my brother had when he was little, and we talked about my mother without either of us crying. I reached over to the dresser and opened the small Chinese music box. Neither of us remembered where or when it was bought, who bought it, or whether it was a gift. In the tiny space lined with red felt was a copper bracelet my father bought for her once in Mobile, Alabama. "She looked good in it," he said, "with her pheasant feather hat." I studied it, fingered it, let it drop back into the music box which played a little Chinese song. "Good night, friend," I said and got up and reached for the light switch.

✳

Saturday morning, first thing, I decide to call Sally, whom I've not seen for a long time. Her roommate answers: "Hold on." I wait. "She's in the bathtub now. Can she call you back?"

"Sure."

I must take a shower. I hop in. My father knocks at the bathroom door and says it's Sally. I shout above the water's noise: "Tell her I'll call her back when I get out of the shower." The hot shower is nice as making love. I finish, wipe myself with the wash cloth so, when I get out, the whole bathroom floor doesn't get wet. My father taught me that.

After drying my hair with a blow dryer, I call Sally. Her roommate says she's on the toilet, can she call me back? "Sure." I think: I wonder if I'll have time to drive to the store and pick up a few groceries. I'm starving.

Returning from the store with milk, bread, and eggs, I learn from Father that Sally called. I call her back. Oh, her roommate says, she had to step out of the house for a few hours. It was an emergency. "What happened?" I ask. "Somehow her mother's bathtub overflowed. She went over to help clean up the mess."

"Oh, I see, thank you." I hang up. This is a crazy world, I think to myself. I'll just call her some other time. What I wanted to talk about wasn't that urgent anyway.

3.

Somehow I sensed, or I saw, as clearly as I could see a cat's eyes in my headlights, that at that moment Mr. Raindrinker couldn't be a writer. But I did not deny him the possibility to change, to accept his life without the immediate gratification he so desperately needed. In the artist's apprenticeship, which may last a lifetime, there is always the chance the art may be ugly to most if not all. And so, it is enough to say: I will not make art from myself because I may not get love in return.

One morning he came to visit me in my study which was half of my bedroom. I could see he was anxious. His eyes were slits. Before he began to speak he sighed and looked away from me. He held his arms tightly over his stomach.

"Is there something you would like to confess?" I asked. "I can assure you that whatever you tell me will remain confidential."

Mr. Raindrinker was not one for self-pity. He was disturbed, but he stuck to pure fact, except when I interrupted to ask how he felt from time to time while he talked. Before he began I had one thought: that in your life, in what you say and do and feel (especially feel, which will show), you may betray yourself to anyone at any time. At any given moment, like art, you may be liked or disliked.

"Last night I woke up," he began. "I knew I was dead. I hugged and pinched myself and just waited for some sign that I was alive. It took a few minutes to realize I was still in and of this world."

"How do you feel now?"

"Sad and afraid."

"Go on."

"I remember when I was twelve. I was in love with Missy Weber. She spent one weekend at the home of her best friend, who was my next door neighbor. I wanted to go over and be with her. But I felt I needed an excuse. How terrible if she knew I loved her! For I knew she couldn't love me. She never even looked at me or talked to me in school. I kept my feelings inside. It hurt. It hurts now in my belly."

I got up and put two chairs facing each other.

"OK, Mr. Raindrinker. Please sit in this chair. Now pretend your belly is in that other chair. I'd like for you to talk to your belly and tell it how you feel."

"That sounds crazy."

"Go ahead. Let me see the actor in you."

He addressed the chair: damn it, belly you've really been a shit to me. All these years you have hurt me. And now you've even infected my bowels. Go to hell, belly!

Go straight to hell!

"How do you feel now?"

"Better."

"You know, I can't help but feel there's still something going on between you and your mother."

"My mother told me I was stupid. Stupid!"

"She's in the chair now. Tell her how you feel about that."

"Mother, you shit, how dare you call me stupid! Bitch!"

There was a long silence. "Is that all you have to tell her today?"

"Yes, that's all."

"Good, what's your belly saying now.?"

"It's not hurting as much."

"What other memories do you have?"

"When I was fifteen, I was alone most of the time. Once, when my parents went shopping on a Saturday, I went exploring into my mother's dresser. I found a brassiere, a panty girdle, and some lipstick. I just had to feel what it was like to wear them. Understand?"

"Sure, go on."

"When I dressed in her things and put the lipstick on, I felt weak between my legs, just like I felt when I stole the bag of coffee from the supermarket."

"How do you feel now?"

"It feels good to talk. I could never tell this to a priest. What would he think of me?"

"Do you still go to church?"

"No. The last time I sat in a pew and kneeled down at a communion rail was for Easter in 1969. I was twenty-seven. That night I dreamed I was falling from a ship into water, and I called out to a priest who was eating supper, but he refused to catch me and break my fall. If he did, he said, his food would get cold."

"That must have been pretty scary."

"It was."

"And your behavior? You wanted to work to change it?"

"Yes."

"OK. I'm sorry, but I can't be of assistance to you any longer. Friend, I'm not a professional at this. A man must have many teachers in his lifetime. To be more concise, I'd advise you to put your money in another bank. I think you might want to talk to a woman now. Is that OK?"
"Of course."

"Keep me posted." I handed him a folded piece of paper with a name, address, and telephone number on it. He shook my hand. I know I will see him again, perhaps changed. It's been a good morning.

4.

Where is my patience? Mr. Raindrinker flew to New York to explore restaurants for a few days. My father wouldn't understand what I had written. But maybe Mr. Raindrinker would. A letter would be too slow, so I send him a telegram to his hotel room. "When I say I am becoming numb to the use of figurative language, I still cannot escape from it. Like the butcher who dislikes eating meat because he sees it all day long, I stiffen at the thought of metaphor and simile, but cannot deny they ease the hunger for language." Later in the day I receive his reply: Don't understand your message. Will be home tomorrow. Talk to you then.

He called me the next day. But my eagerness to tell my thought to anyone had greatly diminished, and, in fact, I was embarrassed at having sent a telegram. I told this to Mr. R. D. over the phone.

"OK," he said, "if you don't want to say anymore about it—"

"I don't. Look, I'll talk to you later."

"By the way, I'm seeing the woman therapist you sent me to."

"Good. How's that going?"

"Fine. But I've only started my work with her. It's going to take some time."

"How was New York?"

"Great. I like discovering my own out-of-the-way working man's restaurants. And, on my own, I searched them out. My last night there I was walking near Michael's Pub, and I thought someone was following me. I turned around to see. Who was it but Woody Allen. I don't remember what we said, but he's real accessible, for someone who's so famous. The only thing I really remember, though, was that I did not ask him for his autograph."

"That's admirable."

"I know. When you meet Raindrinker, you meet someone who's anything but so crass and common as to ask for an autograph."

That morning I fixed scrambled eggs and toast for my father. Then I spent an exciting morning studying biology. I was interested in learning more about how RNA coded for proteins. Having taken the first semester of Biology 101 ten years before, I remembered a story my professor told a whole lecture room full of students. We were studying the excretory and digestive systems in birds. Professor Hawks said the two systems were combined in birds in such a way as to make carrying this load not so heavy, and that gave them easier access to flight. Then he said: "So the next time you open your car door and find on the roof what the birds have left behind, don't curse the poor things out. Rather, just think how wonderful nature really is!"

Ah yes, did I mention I met a girl from Memphis, sunning herself? The whole story ends with us going through the whole in-out-in-out syndrome, the tickling and the rubbing of love. So maybe I'll say it now and get it over with.

Remember how bad a shape Elliot Gould's car was in, in that movie *Getting Straight* where he played a poor graduate student studying in the English Department?

Well, my VW was in almost as bad a shape with its dents everywhere and its burning oil.

Ah, why do people passing in cars blow their horns all the way down the street, as now?

Well, if that's not enough, tomorrow I've got to go down to traffic court and tell the judge I can't pay my speeding ticket cause I'm collecting unemployment and can't afford to pay the damned thing.

But back to the girl from Memphis. First, though, now that it's spring, I'll lead into the story. Many years ago I had tried to put down my thoughts of meeting a young girl. O how terrible my first efforts trying to imitate the German writer Kleist with his long sentences. Yet even he sounded better than me. Here is the first awful paragraph:

"I am twenty-one. The day after my first affair with a young lady I sit shirtless, exposing the scar below my neck from an operation once, facing against the sultry Sunday morning semi-city breeze, on an aluminum lawn chair perched alone atop a wrought iron gray wooden-floored balcony opposite the St. Louis Cathedral, and with my hangover and feelings of guilt I watch the churchgoers, the women who refuse to wear hats, only veils, and the men who carry umbrellas for fear of an impending rain which will probably not come until later in the early afternoon, and after they will have all come home from church." All wrong! All wrong! Full of hyperbole and unable even to breathe. It's worth a good laugh, this school boy's misdirected prose. Never again.

Nevertheless: all morning I've been thinking about how I might have talked to the pretty waitress I saw yesterday in an expensive restaurant. I was treated to lunch. This waitress wore those cute short pants with stockings and heels, and she was less than five feet tall, like my Aunt Sylvia who was the first woman I really began to notice.

I must not be myself. I mean the technique I had to use: wearing a linguistic mask. It was near Lake Pontchartrain, near the well kept lawns and concrete steps leading to the water where I met her. I was getting the first suntan of the year, well, it was April, about eighty degrees, but I wanted to start early. I lay on one of my father's old, stained, white Navy blankets, made about 1943. I was reading Camus and Kafka.

I, slightly overweight, she maybe twenty-one or twenty-two, in a bikini and on her stomach atop a huge beach towel. I introduced myself as Rolf Zander from Düsseldorf. That was enough. I had a good German accent speaking English. The likes and dislikes were my own. I was the one did most of the talking: books and their authors. She must have enjoyed the confident, teacher type in me. She smiled a lot. She did not wear sunglasses, which put me at ease. I wanted to get to know her, but then I was kind of shy. I told her I had to go without asking for her phone number. The only thing I knew was she lived somewhere in the French Quarter.

The next day I met her by accident in a hamburger grill on Royal Street. "Vell, hello, meine Freundin," I said with a heavy German accent. She was smiling. Suddenly I felt relieved. I didn't need Rolf Zander anymore. I confessed to be Kent Soileau from here. I expected she would cry or slap me. No, she laughed out loud. We decided to drive back to the beach together. The gas tank in my oil-burning VW was less than a quarter full, and I had only two dollars in change divided among my four pockets. Sometimes I'll drive around with the needle showing nothing. Talk about laziness, or poverty.

The water at the concrete steps: bubbly froth where it slapped the seawall. Green algae, slippery to walk on, lined the steps. The barnacles looked like chipped teeth with tongues inside them sticking out at us. This lake used to be fresh water. Over the years it had become brackish. Carolyn sneezed herself out of the cold water. She had taken a running-to-a-jump dive, which she did without warning. She smiled. I could see her teeth were all set neatly in their rows and none were crooked.

I told her she had pretty teeth. Something called to her mind the time she lost her front baby teeth and stayed awake to see if the rabbit would bring her money. He never came. Yet she still believed in generous rabbits. "Maybe he just got sick that night," she said with a smirk. I loved her imagination. We swam out for a hundred yards or so. I showed off by doing a perfect backstroke. She splashed water in my face and tried to get away by hiding under the surface. I grabbed her around the waist underwater. Pulled her close to me. Squeezed her breasts. We surfaced. A tin beer can floated by. I snatched it up, squeezed it in one hand, which was difficult but something I'd practiced, since I was a teenager, with my uncle who bragged about his muscles. I set it atop the water, watched it fill and sink.

All around us swimmers were dunking each other so much that the scene resembled a Baptism gone wild. We both casually glanced at a teenager with acne, floating on an old patched-up inner tube, the kind that sand will stick to.

"How do you feel about pimples and braces?" Carolyn asked me.

"I don't know. I guess it's sort of unpleasant to look at." That was not the answer she expected of me.

"Well, I think that those things give a person a chance to build up a resistance to those in society who scorn them for their looks."

"I guess you're right," I mumbled shyly following that deeply felt defense of the unbeautiful. I guess she was getting back at me for my erudition the day before in my German disguise. A sand fly buzzed down onto a drop of water on my arm. It stung. No matter how much I shooed it away, it always came back. Looking up at her, I decided to change the subject.

"One of my friends almost drowned here the other day in this shallow five feet of water."

"Really?" she said, giving me this forced, puzzled look to impress me, I thought. And yet by then she would have already tried to impress me had she intended that. Maybe she was naturally a nice person.

"Yeah, he was in his scuba diving suit and was submerged in shallow water when he heard the sound of an outboard motor. It would have cut him to pieces if he had not lain flat on the sandy bottom of the lake. He said the boat passed directly overhead." Wouldn't you know, it always happens after you gossip over the misfortunes of someone else. I cut my foot, my flat foot on a piece of glass in the sand. It didn't hurt. I felt only a slight pressure piercing my skin. I was one for accidents near water. Once, when I was twelve, my brother's fishing hook got caught in my leg, and it was hell getting it out. On the concrete steps I stood on one foot and lifted the other to see, hopping around on the good foot. The flap of skin winked at me, and then the blood came. Carolyn wiped the blood from my foot, kissed it, and using her fingers put on some kind of lotion she had in her purse. What she did reminded me of Salinger's story, "A Perfect Day For Bananafish." In it Seymore kissed Sybil's arches. My arches, however, were lost in my mother's womb. Why did I feel that every man who stared at Carolyn's unimprisoned breasts was a creep? I limped back to the car in order not to get grass and dirt in the cut.

My friend Charlie Flanagan, an ex-teacher and visual artist, who lived in the Quarter, had given me a key to his apartment before he left town for the weekend. While driving over to Charlie's place, a spell of laughter over some absurd triviality lasted for half an hour between me and Carolyn. We came to a stoplight.

"Do you usually use your gears to slow down your car?" she chuckled. She amused me with her inquisitiveness. She had run away from home in Memphis a few years before because, among other reasons, her parents thought that one of her girlfriends was some sort of pervert.

On Royal Street I couldn't find a place to park so I parked in a loading zone. I knew the cops usually didn't give tickets for loading zones on the weekends.

I pulled Charlie's key out of my jeans' pocket. A penny fell out. I let it stay. Unlocking the door was tricky. I had to juggle the key. Through the long, dark, damp, narrow corridor we walked back to the steps leading to the second floor. Upstairs the place was pretty messy.

We were hungry from swimming. We rummaged through the refrigerator for food, found the bread, mayonnaise, and ham. We picked the fat from the slices of ham and made sandwiches. Actually, she picked the fat, which sort of annoyed me. My parents had brought me up not to waste anything. But my feeling of annoyance lasted only briefly. It was quickly forgotten, and I never said to her: "Gosh, do you really *have* to pick the fat from the ham?" Charlie never kept milk since it upset his stomach. So we drank beer, something he always kept a large supply of.

We decided to repaint the dull yellow ceiling of the apartment, but not the gray walls. Although Charlie, an art teacher, kept all sorts of paints and brushes in his attic, the job required a ladder we didn't have. We had to stand on the bed posts to reach the ceiling. Even that wasn't enough. So Carolyn boosted me up in a precarious position to paint.

All told, less than half the ceiling was painted, even then sloppily. There were skipped spots, paint dripped over the floor, and yellow insects, mostly flies, caught in the spider webs in the corners of the ceiling we painted over. We had no turpentine to clean the brushes. They stiffened. We were tired. We left them on the mantle piece next to the colorful glass menageries, the dusty paperbacks, and the grandfather clock stopped at five o'clock. Charlie won't be angry at us. I just know it.

Outside I can hear an Irish setter chasing every car for a block, and, like a cab looking for more business, it runs back up the block and goes after another car. Poor foolish life of a dog, not even sense enough to stop running in circles. Is there someone watching over you, perhaps the Guardian Angel of Dog?

I pull Carolyn back onto the torn sofa. "Hey look, I'm sorry I forgot to shave. I didn't have time today."

"Don't worry," she says, "we'll kiss without rubbing cheeks."

Now, my friends, I'll put it this way. In 1934 Clark Gable, after having gotten a motel room for himself and Claudette Colbert, hung this blanket over a rope drawn across the room to separate their single beds, their not being married. In the end the walls of Jericho came tumbling down.

I really like that scene, Carolyn, where the imagination sufficed to understand the full implication of what happened. You know, thirty now, and I still close my eyes in the movies these days when the heavy petting starts. And so, kind lady from Memphis, so much has happened since we parted. It took me two months to say: Objects are too important for Americans. I would rather lie in an ocean of family names.

I tended bar for a while at that great jazz place, down the block from Charlie's, with the sad old black bass player you liked so much. If you ever read this, please write.

5.

Before, Mr. Raindrinker had not told me everything about his trip to New York. Now he has some time to do so.

New Orleans International Airport. There was a woman sitting next to him in the huge lobby. Her perfume smelled good. She spoke English to another woman. They both had Scandinavian accents. She yawned. He yawned. He ran his fingers through his hair. He bought a ball point pen from a deaf mute who was smiling. He left his umbrella lying near his seat and went to put a quarter in the coffee machine. He had only turned his back and walked a few hundred feet. He returned. Sat down. Looked around at people. Two girls were popping their chewing gum. Some were smoking. He watched one lady for a long time. Her hand and lip movements, while smoking, were so graceful, so sexy. She tilted her head back to blow the smoke upwards. Then he glanced down on the floor.

Shit! he thought. Where is my umbrella? How could I be so dumb to leave it for someone to steal? This was an airport. People should be affluent here. Shit! he thought again. That thing was expensive.

Mr. Raindrinker told me his flight to New York City was great. It was a clear day, and the pilot announced the cities they flew over: the Mississippi Gulf Coast; Mobile,

Alabama; Atlanta; Richmond, Virginia. In between cities he gazed out the window watching the tiny, winding streams, which were probably rivers, and roads and puzzle-like pieces of land that was America. The stewardesses all smiled serving lunch. He was especially interested in talking to the beautiful woman sitting opposite from him, but she was with someone, though it probably wasn't her husband from the way they talked. Her eyes and the eyes of Mr. R. D. met several times. The plane flew over Washington. He could see the Potomac, the White House, the Capitol, and the Lincoln Memorial. He looked over to the beautiful woman. She was asleep, her head tilted on a pillow against the window. When the plane landed in Newark, they both got up at the same time and met in the aisle. "It's pretty cold outside," he told her nonchalantly, "didn't you bring a coat along?" He was hoping to start a conversation. But she only slightly laughed and looked down. Once in his life silence like this would have hurt. Now he took more risks talking to strangers. And it didn't hurt so much.

It cost fifteen dollars to go to his hotel by cab. But when he got out, he let the cab driver keep the change of a twenty and patted him on the back because the cab driver was a good-natured fellow, who replied with laughter to all Mr. R. D.'s small talk and jokes. The cab driver was named Franz. He was from the Virgin Islands, and his English wasn't too good. He said his native tongue was a patois French.

"Oh, my wife is from Louisiana. New Orleans," he said with an accent. They talked about how good the creole cooking was down there, the filet gumbo, the jambalaya, the andouille, the boudin from Southwest Louisiana, as well as the Muffalata's and the roast beef po-boy sandwiches and the red beans and rice with smoked sausage, all from New Orleans. Franz couldn't make a living in the Virgin Islands. "Tourists, they no more come," he said.

Mr. Raindrinker was amazed they still had bell hops in hotels. He was confused when the bell hop brought his luggage up. At Room 609 he said: "Say, it's been a long time since I been in a hotel. How much should I tip you?" "Oh," the bell hop said, "a dollar is fine." He was a huge man of about fifty. What puzzled Mr. R. D. most was there was no TV in the room. He didn't bother to ask anyone why. He had lost interest in TV a long time ago. No one knew this about him, but every spare moment he took out a book of contemporary poetry. He wanted it kept a secret. He knew no one else who did this, except for Soileau. Again and again he asked himself: who in the hell reads American poetry in America anyway? You have to be emotionally disturbed to write it and a sissy to read it. That's what most people think, he thought. Across town in a tiny hospital a great American poet born in 1927 in Ohio was passing from his life. At 7:30 on the night of March 18th, Mr. Raindrinker, knowing not a soul in New York, walked three blocks to the Guggenheim Museum to hear a Rhode Island-born poet pay tribute to his favorite poet from Ohio. During the reading he thought: Martin's Ferry, Ohio will be saddened, but how can a country that mostly doesn't read poetry be saddened? How can a country with the millions of tiny green and brown squares in it he saw from the airplane be sad? Did the stars blink equally as much for the great deaths as for the many small deaths? Give this man the whorehouses in Wheeling, West Virginia and the great whales, who can no longer find each other even to mate. Give him the beautiful guts of a porcupine shot by a Vermont woodsman, and hanging by them from a branch. Give him the winter roads that end in nothing but trees, for that is the road you will find him on.

In the middle of the poetry reading, Mr. R. D.'s eyes watered up, and he walked out into a snowy night with only a light jacket. He was cold. His head was filled with poems, or at least only fragments of poems, but he couldn't write. And then Soileau had called him a dilettante, and that didn't help. All he had in his head was a fragment:

> *Children knew it;*
> *Thickened gumbo is the best gumbo.*
> *Toes are to number like pigeons.*
> *One toe, two toes.*
> *The dead count on the living to bury them.*

He went into a small restaurant near 86th and Madison Avenue. He was shown a table by a waiter in a green vest. He could see the fresh meats and the fresh desserts in the glass case. How fast the service is here in this kind of restaurant, he thought, compared to the South. Is the waiter rushing me to make room for others, or does he sense I'm in a hurry and is trying to accommodate my haste, or the haste of any New Yorker for that matter? Does it show I'm anxious?

At the next table only inches from him he heard a man talking to his wife: "Mother's life is a wreck, Jerry's life is a wreck, so what's the difference if we tell them both to move out?"

He wanted to talk to someone, anyone. He smiled and introduced himself to the New Yorker. "Hi! I'm from New Orleans. I overheard you had a small business. I own a small print shop myself." He said that just because he couldn't really think of what he was doing at the moment.

"Oh, from New Orleans? You don't sound like you're from there," the New Yorker said, and his wife smiled.

"Well, you see New Orleans has many accents, but the most notable one is called "yat." It comes from people who say "Where y'at?" in the ninth ward of the city. It's close to the Al Smith inflection in Hoboken. In my own case I studied foreign languages in college, which sort of neutralized my New Orleans accent. Some people tell me I sound like I speak with a radio announcer's speech."

"Yeah, your accent is kind of neutral."

"Oh, thanks," Mr. R. D. laughed nervously, looked down, and took a bite of his corned beef sandwich on rye.

"Yeah," said the New Yorker, "inflation is killing my small business."

"Me, too. My printing business is in bad shape. I may have to declare bankruptcy." There was a girl on the other side of him who had a misshapen forehead, and who let half a bottle of catsup dribble onto her French fries. Her mother said: "Keep up that shit and you won't watch TV when we get home."

"Well, it was nice meeting you," the New Yorker said, picked up his check, and shook Raindrinker's hand. His wife smiled.

Mr. R. D. drank only half his cup of coffee. He felt sad. He thought again about the poet from Ohio who wrote of President Harding and horses nuzzling the poet's hand. Perhaps even now his body was entering into the blossom of his next life.

In his mind Mr. R. D. was not quite satisfied with his fragment, so he rethought it, as a drunk was beating on the subway doors.

You've known it all along:

add water and soup begets itself.
Toes are to name, like orphans.
The already dead are alive, only poor.

And he left New York.

6.

There was a party across the street. The guy whose parents gave him the house: I knew him since he was a little kid. I must have been six or seven years older. He was just getting a divorce. I guess the party was helping to fill his otherwise empty life.

With the rain I could no longer hear the voices of the party goers. They had all left the front lawn and gone inside. It started raining really hard. This was Friday night, and the rain didn't let up till Sunday noon. All next day and night, thunder shook the windows. The lightning reminded me of the man I saw on TV, who was struck by lightning seven different times and lived to tell it. Now that was an exception.

Sunday afternoon on TV they said most of the city experienced flooding. My father and I were lucky living near Highway 90, the highest spot in Orleans Parish. Much of New Orleans didn't drain well because much of it was just below sea level, and the city's pumping system was too outdated to keep up with the quickly rising water. They showed film of cars parked on the streets, underwater. It was pretty sad. The water was level with the doorstep of this one house, and a car passing in the street made just enough waves for the water to seep under the door into the house. Perhaps the furniture was feeling unwelcome, like partygoers, who have stayed really too late into the night.

In the rain I daydream. Sure, I'd like to be a famous news announcer because everyone hears you telling the truth. I do an impression of Paul Harvey.

"In a moment, after a few words from our sponsor, more of today's news with Kent Soileau. (Pause.) Good evening again. Page Two. A man from Norway. A girl, nineteen, from Canada. Both hitchhike to Louisiana, where he gets a job as a lumberjack. His first paycheck and they go out to eat at the finest restaurant in Baton Rouge. They take a walk behind an apartment complex. Suddenly from the dark, a man opens fire with a small caliber pistol. Shot in a foreign country. He is now unconscious in the hospital. A bullet is lodged in her spine. She is paralyzed from the waist down. Police say the man who shot them thought for sure she was his wife with another man. They looked exactly alike. O the tragedy of the double! Today is her birthday. And that's the news. Good (pause) day! ("Day" is said with a rising inflection.)

Actually I prefer the way the Germans say it. We say: It's a small world. But the Germans make the metaphor. They say: *Die Welt ist ein Dorf.* Or: the world is a small town.

Anyway, I'm standing at the bar making a frozen strawberry daiquiri for this waitress I've gotten to know, who brings her personal problems to work. She's telling me, well, you know how people tell you something serious and sort of laugh about it, probably to try to ease the pain for both the speaker and the listener. This is Lisa. She confides in me. All the waitresses do. What's it, do I resemble a psychiatrist? She's busy so she doesn't have time to finish telling me about her husband. "I'll talk to you later," and she scurries away.

Let's see. I said that the world is a small town. Right. Two guys walk up to the bar and ask what brand of beer we have. I tell them.

"OK. Two drafts," they say simultaneously.

One looks at me: "Say, have there been any murders lately here on Bourbon Street?"

"Why, sir?"

"Well, we just ducked in here."

"Don't tell me. Two guys were following you."

"Yeah, how'd ya know?"

"You looked nervous."

"Do you think I'm being paranoid?"

"Well, sir, do you see anybody out there?"

The two men in business suits look out the big window in front of Li'l Momma's Restaurant and Bar.

"No, I don't see 'em," says the one that's doing the talking.

"Well, just stay in here for a while. If you recognize them, I'll just call the cops."

All of us heard sirens. Five fire trucks and a hook-and-ladder came to a whining stop in the next block. Several people got up from their meals and walked out the front door to see what was going on.

"What's that?" one of the men in a business suit asks me.

"Oh," I say coolly, "a five alarm fire. Happens all the time in the Quarter. This is just a false alarm I'm sure. Probably some guy was barbecuing on his balcony, some drunk saw more smoke than he was used to, hit an alarm, and caused all the commotion. But it's best to err on the side of caution. If there really was a fire in the Quarter, the buildings are so close together that a whole block would go up in flames in a matter of minutes. That explains all those fire trucks bustin' ass to get here."

I could see a fully dressed fireman, axe in hand, resignedly hop back on the truck. I just know that dude wanted some action this time. To many firemen a false alarm is almost like hearing your mother died. To them it's the feeling a woman who wants to get pregnant has when her lover withdraws just before that incredible explosion. It took quite a while for them to leave. Before long the street, whose very name was indigenously American whiskey, again resembled schools of fish going in opposite directions.

"Been workin' here long?" the short man asks me.

"No, not long."

"Sounds like you know this area pretty well."

"Well, I was born in this town, but I never imagined I'd be workin' in a bar on Bourbon Street. Hell, most of my friends avoid the place. One friend calls it a clean, well-lit slum. I mean do New Yorkers go to see the Statue of Liberty? Same difference for New Orleaneans. But I like it here OK, to tell you the truth."

The short man lights a cigarette. "Would you pass me that ashtray?"

"Sure." I begin again: "You fellas here visitin'?"

"No," the man who's hardly said anything till now says, "on a business trip."

Now I know geography, and sometimes on the throne in the morning I'll seriously look through an atlas of the U. S. So I know about three or four towns in every state I can mention. I love to read maps on the toilet. I wonder if Lyndon Johnson ever read a map on the toilet?

"Where ya from?"

"Midwest." Pause. "Nebraska."

"Oh, really? I have a friend in Lincoln. He works in a library up there."

Both their faces light up. "Hey, man, *we're* from Lincoln. What's your friend's name?"

"Sears. Bill Sears. He works in the serials department of the university library." I'm not kidding. I really do know a guy there, the only person in Nebraska I *do* know.

One man turns to the other, his voice excited. "Hey, Fred. Ole Bob Johnson works at that library. He just might know this bartender's friend. Damn, we'll have to ask him when we get back."

"Damn right."

"What business y'all in?" I really say *y'all* sometimes. Sometimes it slips out. I used to be self-conscious about saying "y'all" to anyone not from the South, but now I kind of like that mellifluous Southernism.

"We work for the Lincoln Book Company. We buy back recent editions of textbooks the students use in college."

Then it hits me. Once, a few years ago, still a student, I worked in the bookstore at Tulane University uptown. But that story will be in a personal essay of mine someday. Anyway, I sure as hell recognize this guy.

"Say," I said, "you didn't know Bill Conroy who was textbook manager at Tulane about 1970, did ya?"

"Why, I sure did. He worked with Melinda—"

"Melinda Phillips," I say, excited.

"Yeah, that's right. Wow! You know Bill's in Waco now. Textbook manager at Baylor. A damned good job."

To me the word *good job* is an oxymoron. Then "a-damned-good-job-what-the-hell-do-I-know-about-damned-good-jobs" flashes through my mind.

I can't help but continue with all this: "Well, so how is he? Did he get married to the girl he was dating? Does he still drive that, what the hell's the name of that Swedish sports car?"

"Yeah, he's married now. And he still drives a Saab, only a newer one." And for one instant I think about my oil-leaking, dented, generally fucked up Volkswagen.

"Well, I'll be," the shorter man says. "We saw him last week when we were in Waco. He's still the same great, easy-going guy." Surprised a waiter or waitress hadn't come up to the bar for me to make them a drink, I say, "Bill and I worked, as you can probably guess, for a year together in New Orleans at Tulane. I remember you now. Several years ago you did business with our bookstore."

Each of them reaches out his hand, and I shake each one. The shorter man says, "What's your name, anyway?"

"Kent."

"Kent? With a "t"?

"Yeah," I give out an embarrassed sort of chuckle and look down. "Kent Soileau. It's a Cajun French surname."

"Oh, I see." He takes out a pad from the inside pocket of his suit coat and begins to write. "How ya spell that?"

I say patiently: "S-O-I-L-E-A-U."

"Well, we'll see Bill Conroy again on our way back up to Nebraska. We'll tell him we saw you, of all places on Bourbon Street."

"Excellent. Tell him I think of him from time to time. A real good manager. You know he's from Ponca City, Oklahoma."

"Right."

"I wondered what happened to— ." There's a knock on the front glass by the bar. Two pretty ladies in stunning outfits are waving at my two newly discovered acquaintances. Real great guys. Cosmopolitan, I think, yet down home. "Say we gotta go. Our wives finally found us."

They gulp down the rest of their beer.

I wink at them: "Remember, if you see those guys following you, I can always call the cops."

One winks back: "That's OK. Our wives will protect us now." They laugh. I laugh.

They leave me a five dollar tip. Damn I felt unusually cheerful, not only because of the tip, but, well, all of us living far apart, and we know one fantastic guy from out of all of our past. Funny thing is I never got around to asking them their names.

Later I tell this one waitress Sybil: "Sybil, where is your prince? Don't tell me. He was handsome, but no money or feelings. No, he wasn't handsome, but had money and plenty of feelings. No, he wasn't handsome, had no money, and absolutely no feelings, which means he could never be the star of a TV show." I've got Sybil in stitches. Flirting and kidding around is great. I like it. Sybil likes it. Only the manager doesn't like it. He doesn't approve of employees flirting on company time. I really think he's jealous of me.

They hired me here because I convinced them I was a bartender from a bar that closed in another city, and I moved down to New Orleans. But I know my stuff. For the past two years I been memorizing how to mix drinks on my own. Got a good book on it. Sometimes during the day I would go through a drink in my mind.

A gimlet. A gimlet, I think. What's in it? OK. Brandy, no that's a Stinger. Gin. 1 ½ ounces of that. One more ingredient. Kahlua. No. Shit. What? Lime juice. ½ ounce of that. How is it served? On the rocks, in a rocks glass. And this thought comes to me faster: garnish with a lime. Put one hand behind the lime so you don't squeeze it all over the customer. Common sense. I would feel pretty proud of myself. How could a brain recall not only sequence, but quantity and ingredient as well?

I don't recall what I was thinking before a song broke from my lips. I am home late Friday night. Can't sleep again. I look in my drawer at a group picture. Sixth grade. I am the only one in the front row standing on the sides of my shoes. I look young for my age compared to the others. Miss Jenny is about 32. Athletic-looking. Big shoulders. Hair cut like a man's. I remember her unusually deep voice and her tennis rackets leaning in the corner of the classroom. Some of us smile. Some don't. I still remember a few of their names.

The old man is asleep. It's now 1 AM Saturday. Well, what about the old man? He used to read the morning paper every morning on the throne. He doesn't anymore. He used to watch the fights on TV when I was a kid. Now he says: "Prizefighting is brutal." He used to work in his woodworking shop. Now his saw blades are rusting away. If his life is changing, what is his next change?

Once my father sang the song of the poker player:

> *I will leave this world*
> *smiling only on the inside.*
> *I will be holding two aces, three jacks.*
> *It will be good enough to win.*
> *I am sure of it.*
> *Good enough to win.*

My father no longer plays cards. Ever since Mother died.

7.

I got to work at Li'l Momma's — after it took me a long time to find a parking place in the Quarter — in my black bow tie, red vest, black pants, and white shirt. I found out I wasn't scheduled to work Monday night. What they had never told me was they change the schedules every week to give everybody a chance to make tips on the weekends, which were usually the busiest. Later, I drove uptown in order to visit the Rusty Nail. On the way I picked up a hitchhiker. He was pretty dirty, wearing jeans and a work shirt. He got in with a newspaper. "First news I've read in two weeks. You see, I work twelve hours a day in a shipyard and don't have a TV, so the last thing I heard about the world was two weeks ago. Same old depressing news, that volcano Saint Helen's erupting in the West sending volcanic ash thousands of feet up into the atmosphere. They say it settled on towns hundreds of miles away. And a race riot in Miami. Same old shit really."

I let him off at Napoleon and St. Charles. He thanked me. I headed toward Cohn Street where an old college buddy lived. I found his house, got out, knocked, but no one was home. Some streets in New Orleans have these little concrete culverts that make a drainage ditch next to the driveway, and you can back one wheel in it and get stuck, so you can't get out unless someone helps you pull it out. It happened to me. Fortunately a guy and his girlfriend coming out of his house saw my predicament and offered to help. The guy hitched a chain from my front axle to the trailer hitch of his car and pulled me out. We talked awhile after that. Turned out they know my friend from Tulane, Joe Bradley, whom I hadn't seen in years, but had come to see. I hugged the woman, Terry, and shook Gary's hand. Cheez, I had two dollars in my pocket, certainly not enough to pay for a tow truck to pull me out. Those two gentle folks renewed my faith in people I hadn't felt in a long time.

It was 7 PM. There was only one person drinking at the Rusty Nail Bar, and the bartender, who happened to have little to say to me that night. I drove home and spent the whole night reading Georg Groddeck's *Book of the It*. I just couldn't fall asleep.

While I was finishing my first week behind the service bar at Li'l Momma's, the Drinker of Rain decided to buy himself a motorcycle and leave town. He went up to Baton Rouge to look for work. The best he could get was a job in an all night food store.

He said he eventually got his ass outa Baton Rouge. He just knew the guy who put a gun to his head might have come looking for him if he stayed, since he called the cops after the robbery.

He stayed in Baton Rouge, well, this Friday it would be two weeks. When he came back, he filed this report with me. I mean the Drinker of Rain, who is cousin to the Eater of Snow, can write as well as I can, sometimes, again, when he could accept his life without the immediate gratification of love he so desperately needed.

Cast

Mr. R.D.	*Loser of jobs and women.*
Tenor Masterson	*A dark black manager of Fill-a-Sack store #25, an ex-Air Force sergeant, retired after twenty years.*
Frank Little	*A light black real estate salesman from Detroit. He and Masterson are old Air Force buddies.*
Mr. White	*A tall, thin Negro World War I veteran.*

Maggie   *An eighteen-year-old student living
alone in a large six-room house.*

I was about to ring up the tax on a one dollar sale. I looked at Maggie. Her eyes were soft, and her nose tiny, and her skin a light black. Also she was young and without complaints about prices. I guess her soft eyes did it cause I decided she didn't deserve to pay tax, for that matter no one did. The drawer of the cash register shot out the way a one-armed bandit would if you hit the jackpot, and I felt generous as Robin Hood.

She pushed the money gently toward me, and I scraped off the counter all except four cents. She smiled and was about to correct my mistake, but I put my finger over my lips, and my eyes followed her through the glass of the automatic sliding glass doors, which let out a sigh louder than I could have.

I closed my drawer and looked for Masterson. He popped up like toast from behind the slurpee machine.

"Some ass, huh," I said. He said nothing. His rag was getting at the hard-to-reach places on the slurpee machine where cherry crystals filled a cup that made any kid's day. I didn't like the silence.

"Well, gee, can't a trainee even look at girls?"

"That's not the point, Chief," he said, really overdoing his job cleaning up, I thought.

"Chief, didn't you forget to ring up tax?" he asked, forcing a smile.

"Tax? I didn't know there was tax on toilet paper. I mean the stuff's expensive enough already."

"That's not the point, Chief. But if you didn't know, remember for the next time." Then he added an "OK?" just before the last stroke of his clean-up job, plopped rag in bucket, and walked slowly to the back room where the sink was.

Frank Little came in the door laughing. He was always laughing about something. He was short, chubby, sold real estate, told tremendously funny stories, and I liked him, even though I'd only known him for a week.

"How's the new trainee?" he said, giggling a pleasant giggle. I didn't answer him, just raised my eyebrows, and he giggled some more.

Major and his sisters with braided hair were all taking their sweet time by the long aisle of nickel and penny candies. The girls finally paid for what they wanted, but Major, who was about waist high to any grown-up, kept looking. When he looked up to see his sisters gone, he shot out the door, yelling "Hey, wait for me!"

I kind of laughed at that little fart Major who got left behind. He must have come in the store thirty times a day for a handful of penny candies, always plopping down on the counter less money than he owed me, and I, I'm telling him, sorry Major, but that ain't enough. So he'll put some back, slouching toward the candy shelf so that I can never tell whether he is angry or just happy I didn't tell him to put even more candy back on the rack.

I saw Masterson coming out of the back room from working bottles, and knowing how Frank Little had just written our store a bad check, I asked Masterson, "Is this guy's credit good here?" Little laughed. Masterson said: "Uh, uh, nope, Chief, send him down the street. Let him do business with some other store." Little laughed, but then got serious by saying it was the bank's fault, still we said we would never let him off the hook, and we all laughed again.

Little huddled us over the counter and told us the one

about three men of God, an Irish priest, a black Baptist preacher, and a Rabbi who were fishing in a boat, and the preacher and the Rabbi forgot the bait so they walked over water back to shore. The priest was amazed, and thought he'd try it, but went plop and sunk. The preacher tells the Rabbi, "You think we oughta tell that fool where the rocks were?" I had heard that story once before, except when I heard it the black preacher went swimming, not the priest.

"You know how I heard that story, don't ya?" I put it to Little. He thought a second, then giggled.

Masterson went to the back room. I stepped out from behind the counter, and in front of Little I walked hunched over like Masterson, and began talking just like him, using that word he always uses, Chief. Little was laughing.

Little cupped his hand sideways to his mouth and yelled to the back room, "Hey, Sarge, you still givin' this nice young white boy a hard time?" Frank called me a boy, and I guess he wouldn't have believed me if I told him I was thirty-five.

Masterson came in from the back with a stiff-shouldered walk and said, "Don't you never mind, Little, you know what a goof off you were in the service. Don't be givin' my assistant manager any ideas about adoptin' your ways."

Masterson said he was in the mood for a soda. Little reluctantly dug in his pockets for change. Masterson was a clever store manager. He bought sodas for all his women customers and made all his so-called buddies feel like it was always their turn to owe him one. It all balanced out in the end, I guessed. Actually I felt uncomfortable about saying "soda", being from New Orleans where they said either "soft drink" or, if you were from the country towns around New Orleans, they said "pop." But I said "soda" anyway so they wouldn't think I was a total stranger. Actually I was pretty good at using red-neck Baton Rouge expressions just enough so it didn't sound like I was overdoing it.

Mr. White walked in from preaching. He always got the same cold drink—there, there's another way to say it—a Dr. Pepper. He had two lower front teeth left. They bobbed continually to the rhythm of his jaw. He was thin, walked with a cane, and wore a straw hat. His black tie with its small knot showed around his thin collar that would not stay down. On his lapel, several pins from the American Legion that bore numbers for years of membership and service.

He set his money down for the drink very carefully, as if it were his whole life's savings. Masterson, with that cruelly-kind streak in him, jostled the old man's hand and grinned to Little and jerked away a dime more than the old soldier owed him. Mr. White's head was still down. He began to shake all over and beat his cane gently against the floor and spoke stuttering and nervous. Theirs was a cruel friendship.

"Now, young man, you really ought not have done that. You, you, y-, y- know, say you know I don't like to fool around when it comes to countin' my money. Now put, I say put my money back down."

Little giggled, and Mr. White was about to walk out hurt and pouting when Masterson, serious as hell, put his arm around Mr. White. "Now, sir, you know we been friends for years, and I wouldn't do nothin' in the world to hurt you. In fact, if you looked carefully, I done give you back your dime."

The old soldier was reluctant to admit to anything. He kept stuttering and bowing and muttering things about the good Lord knows what's right.

That night I worked alone. Just before midnight, at the end of my shift, the most beautiful young black man I ever saw pulled a .38 that demanded money, and somehow, twice I thought about Mr. White stuttering and bowing before Masterson, shell-shocked, like a conquered warrior.

I ran into Mr. Raindrinker again at the Rusty Nail one weekday night, just after it had rained all day but stopped. Bent over a beer, he told me his Dad was just diagnosed with pancreatic cancer, which meant the outcome of the disease was to be quickly fatal. R. D. lost his mother the previous year.

"I got along well with my Dad," he said. "He was a guy who never complained, never let anything bother him, always had a laugh for someone, was never sad, and never lonely because he always had my mother around. I rarely see people like him. Fought in World War II at the Battle of the Bulge, confident the U.S. would win. He said of his experience as a soldier that a bullet was never made with his name on it. All his working life he repaired lawn mowers for Sears and Roebuck at their shop on Jefferson Highway. He knew lawn mowers so well that friends would often ask him to work on theirs, and, being the saint he was, he'd never charge them, or he'd say 'No trouble. Maybe someday you'll do *me* a favor.' Once, in 1945, he was hunkered down in a foxhole with his Company under heavy fire. A German artillery shell hit right behind his best buddy who died immediately from the shock of the shell hitting, but which didn't explode. That's how close he was to death. Ever since then he felt nothing in life to be insurmountable. Soileau, I really already miss him. What will I do knowing the flame of a friendship, a mutual love, cannot be lit again? Raindrinker passed his fingers over his eyes, his head down, took a handkerchief from his back pocket, and wiped.

"I'm sorry, my friend. I'm sorry." And I walked out into the night that seemed darker than usual.

Chapter Eight

1.

Early afternoon. The sleeping medicine I got from a psychiatrist must have worked. I woke up late, having opened my eyes earlier, but went back to sleep. I was due at work at five. I shaved, washed up, and dressed. I couldn't get my right pants' leg on, and I hopped around saying "shit." I fell. But that was good. I needed steady ground to pull on the pants.

My car was parked out front. I had to put some more oil in the damned thing. It burned a quart of oil every 85 miles. Bad piston rings. I kept a supply of cheap oil in the back seat.

Across the street I could see a pack of stray dogs gathered at the front steps of the Stevens' house. They were barking. In the doorway, Melissa, the ten-year-old black Stevens' girl, was yelling at me across the street: "Hey, Mr. Kent, make these dogs go away, please! I wanna go play." I picked up a stick and chased them away. "Thanks," she said passing me quickly, running down the block to meet her girlfriends.

I liked Melissa. I wanted her feelings. Where is the

little boy who drove with his Dad from New Orleans to see in Montauk, Long Island, the house of Grover Cleveland almost no one else could find? Melissa, let me feel like I felt on my first day fishing, ten years old, the first light breaking, in the world of my father's thirty-five years on earth.

The next morning I borrowed Raindrinker's motorcycle. I was looking for a girl I met in a bar on Bourbon Street, right before I went to work. Her name was Melinda. Sketchy details. I only talked to her for ten minutes, then I had to get to work. She was from south of Fresno, California, couldn't hold a waitressing job, was beautiful, twenty-one, confused, and living someplace in the Quarter off the money her grandfather willed her. She promised she'd meet me after I got off work to go Cajun dancing. She wanted me to teach her to waltz most of all. Also she wanted to learn the two-step. I waited an hour longer than the time we agreed to meet. No Melinda. The only thing I know is she mentioned something about getting a job at the State School for the Learning Handicapped. That was my only lead. It's sad, sad.

Just as you walk into the State School for the Learning Handicapped, there's a giant dining room with maybe twenty or thirty tables with ten chairs apiece. In the corner a chubby black girl was coloring. Her face and her jowls looked swollen. Later I realized her pink, tattered chiffon dress bulged heavily at the waistline. Her finger was pointing to her mouth as she was about to choose from the crayons strewn about, some broken, some whole, but all worn down so each stroke made a fat line.

My shielded cycle helmet was still on, even as she called me over to her, and everything, crayons, the flower print on all the tables, the cuckoo clock, the steps, everything, looked blue.

"Hi, come color with me."

I hadn't colored in a long time, and I wasn't in the mood because I had come to see Melinda, even though I knew it was a long shot she worked here. I took off my helmet and backpack, and, in this room full of empty chairs, I took the chair at the head of the table, next to hers on my left.

She was left-handed and was struggling with her printing. "Is this the way you make an 'A'?" she asked me. She was missing a piece of the "A" so I showed her, filling it in. Then she labeled the picture: A HOUSE. She thought a second, scratched out the letter "A", and wrote MY over it. Before I could ask her why she changed her mind, she quickly said: "This is my house."

"You mean the one in the picture."

"Yes, that one, but I mean the one we're sitting in now. It's my house and nobody else's."

The idea of reminding her that the house belonged to the state school occurred to me, but the explanation seemed long and involved, so I only thought about changing the subject. She quickly forgot her topic of ownership.

"You can draw a picture, and if you mess up, you can use the back."

She was well ahead of her time in her thoughts of conserving paper. I looked curiously at her house. It was done in a brown outline, showing just a simple facade of a rectangle beneath a triangle, but the door was very tiny and the windows were up high in the corners. No smoke came from the chimney. It leaned, too, as if in a strong wind.

"How about a sun?" I suggested. "Here, have this yellow."

"No, I don't like yellow," she said rather violently. But then her facial expression changed and she smiled, put her head down, tossing it around, and still smiled. She said: Oh, I do like yellow. It was just a joke when I said I didn't. Did you get the joke?"

I didn't think it was any joke, and I politely said so, still not completely feeling sure if I said the right thing. Several times she hooked me by saying something I least expected, and then quickly said the opposite, and how it was all a joke. I wondered where she learned that. I thought about asking. Yet she was quicker with questions than I was.

"Hey, are you just going to sit there, or are you going to help me color?"

"Sure," I said. She pulled out an orange crayon, not hearing my reply, and was already making the circle and the dashes for rays. She filled in the sun orange and added red and other colors that didn't belong, very violently, caking them on top of one another until the sun was a strange dark mixture. Only the rays of light stayed yellow.

She wanted me to draw a house of my own, only at first I thought she said horse—it came out like "hoss"— so I helped her to say house, and I learned she confused one word for the other, "horse" instead of "house" and the other way around. Her suggestion of "horse" made me change my drawing mid-way to a barn. I had drawn a three-dimensional figure in perspective, in red, added a roof, some big doors in front, and a loft with some hay. I was tempted to do the usual red barn with a brown roof, then decided that as long as the basic barn was there, along with her irregular sun, I could be different. So I gave her a barn painted purple, red, blue, green, brown, orange, and yellow. I thought it would please her, but she was practical with my barn.

"That's not the way a barn should look," she said, and almost as quickly changed her mind, "but I like it." She put some blue clouds and a sun.

I looked up. Outside the clouds were gathering black. I realized that minutes ago, when I walked in, I was in a hurry. I grew uneasy about the weather.

"Nice meeting you, but I have to go. What was your name again?'

"It's Gloria. And can't you stay awhile?"

"Sorry, but I have to get going." Even as my foot scraped clumsily against the mat that said WELCOME, I was thinking about her and what her houses could have meant. "Have a good time," I called back.

I put on my helmet with the blue visor. The sky was blue, even the clouds were light blue. I wasn't thinking what I was doing. A dozen people must have passed before I noticed my helmet on and my friend's motorcycle still two blocks away. A lady turned back to look. I yanked off my helmet. The sky was black with billowing clouds. I felt clumsy.

By Third Street a light drizzle fell. Rainbows of red and purple and green and yellow came out of the black asphalt in patches. Oil mixed with water. In a little while the drizzling stopped. I rode the cycle all day, all over, dressed in the wind, the wind wild, tight-fitting as the water in the shower.

When you're on a cycle, you find out who your friends are. You're a good dancer. It's a party at a huge barn out in the country near Hammond. All the girls you know at your job are there. It's bad to mix tequila and beer, but who doesn't? The best band for miles around is there. They play songs anyone can dance to. You almost pick up a girl who likes the way you dance, but the girl you want to take home has decided to go home with someone else. She doesn't say, though you think she's afraid cause you've turned over once on your motorcycle. And that's cause it's a gravel road outside, and you've had a few tequilas. So you show off your dancing, pick up a girl saying she's getting a divorce from her husband who's up north in Baltimore. She's cute. You ask no further questions. You look around. The party's over, shit. You ask her to go skinny dipping in the bayou nearby. It's 2 AM. You both have jobs the next day. She's got a ride home with friends. You strike out, nevertheless you go skinny dipping by yourself anyway.

When you're drunk, and everyone has left the party in the country except you, you're lonely. It's forty miles back to town. All you have between your legs is a motor and two wheels. It's your only friend. You kiss it again and again, half-naked, alone, and bare-footed after swimming in what you were born in. There are miles and miles and miles. You finally get home, kissing your cycle like a lover.

2.

About noon at Raindrinker's apartment in the French Quarter, I knocked on the door but got no answer. I turned the door knob, finding it not locked. I was embarrassed to see him and his wife naked, in an embrace on the living room floor at their shotgun apartment. R. D. said, "Oh, hi Kent." I guess they wanted to just be spontaneous. "Sorry, you two," I said, quickly closing the door, and: "Keep in touch."

A week later I returned in the early evening. Children

rode past me on their tricycles. Judy had invited me to dinner. The door now opened, I found R. D. pacing. He was unable to stop moving around. All he said to me was a lackluster "hi" and walked back to other rooms. Later he reappeared.

"Honey, would you set the table?"

"Fuck no, that's women's work."

I intruded, "I'll do it, Judy."

"Soileau," he pointed at me violently, "you just sit where you are, cause if you move, I'll kick your ass!"

Judy and I looked at each other questioningly, with raised eyebrows and lifted shoulders.

"Uh – Honey, I'm going to get a small rose tattoo on my ankle. I know you like roses."

"Well that's just fucking great! Why don't you get a hundred more and then you could join the goddamn circus!"

In the uncomfortable silence she said, "Sweetie, why don't you relax and sit down. I'm about to serve dinner."

He picked up a glass from the table and smashed it against the wall. "Screw dinner, I'm going to the bar." Then he walked to the living room and slammed the front door behind him.

Judy was wearing a gold silk blouse; blue culottes; high heels with only a front strap over the toes and no straps on the back, so that the shoes flopped a little when she walked. Not unattractive in pink lipstick, she had what might euphemistically be called a full figure.

"Kent, what are you going to do with a man like that?"

"How long has he been this way?"

"Ever since he found out his father had pancreatic cancer. The only time he calms down even a little is when we make love, and still he has a difficult time keeping an erection. I can't take it anymore. Some nights I can't sleep, I'm so afraid. And he hasn't been doing the routine things around the house he used to do, like take out the garbage. Once I asked him to slice some tomatoes and all he said was *Fear is the enemy of work.*"

"Where's the baby?"

"At my mother's. I can't leave the poor child here with him being that way. I think I'm gonna move to my mother's too." Her hands were visibly shaking as she lit a cigarette. And I never even knew her to be a smoker.

3.

Right next to Li'l Momma's, the man who calls out "show time," and shuts, then opens the door for a peek as the girlies strip tease, says he's gonna have to close his place down. He comes in Li'l Momma's sometimes to get coffee. Every time he talks to me it's about the Russian Revolution and the Russian peasants and Hitler. He says if his girls turn a trick one night and make two hundred dollars, they don't show up for work for many days to dance in their birthday suits.

Anyway, the eyes of the black dudes who work here shine. Especially Willie's eyes. But Shelton, and Chick, and Robbie Malone, those black dudes' eyes shine, too. Willie is the fastest oyster shucker I ever met. He can shuck a dozen oysters a minute, ready for a customer to eat them raw. Tonight I eavesdropped on all the black dudes in the kitchen. Willie was mad at Shelton and called him a bad nigger. Willie said: "Shelton, did your daddy bring you up to say 'yes suh' to the white boss? Well, I likes my boss, and I likes to work in this restaurant, and you betta get off yo black ass and quit foolin' around. When them whores stuck their heads in the restaurant, you and Chick and Robbie was all flashin' your money and sayin' *Baby, I'd like to buy you a drink* and such as *Baby, I wants to get to know you personally*. If the manager would have seen you gawkin' at dem whores like geese, he'd a fired you fo sho."

Sometimes Willie talks to himself, and at times when he talks to me, he mumbles so I can't always understand him. Today I told Willie who's nineteen, a year older than the others, to tell Shelton, Chick, and Robbie, the bus boys, to "go to their room" if they misbehaved.

"Is dat what you tell yo kids, Kent?" Willie asked.

"No, I don't have any kids. About ten years ago a teenage comedian told me that. It was pretty funny. You think it's funny?"

"Yeah, man," Willie said. Next day he told me: "All de times I be tellin' ma friends dat 'go to your room' dey all be laughin'."

I knew what kind of humor Willie could use on his younger friends. "Say, Willie," I said, "if you really want to get a laugh, tell Shelton in front of everybody, say, Shelton you got a face only a mother could love." Willie liked it. I don't believe in putting people down, but you have to understand that's the kind of grim humor those black dudes liked to use on each other. Even bad-assed white dudes liked it.

Business has been slow. Once, four sisters from Germany couldn't order in English, so I had to interpret between them and the waitress. This restaurant, I gather, is losing a lot of money. Most restaurants do when they first open. Or so the manager tells me. He just had some personalized business cards printed up. One of the waiters, Mitch, scratched out the word MANAGER on ten or fifteen of the manager's cards and filled in his own name with SPIRITUAL ADVISER AND PROPHET below it. He handed them all out to customers.

I was getting tired of watching people pass by my window on Bourbon Street by the thousands, but not that so much as listening to the same song every night across the street at the Golden Devil. The singer would sing every night: "She wants a big butter- and-egg-man. Does some big butter-and-egg-man want her?" And: "Hello, central, give me Doctor Jazz." Remember, if you're a bartender in a tourist town where you see someone different every night, you can tell the same jokes and get away with it. Why do people walk up and down Bourbon Street? Are they in the midst of a great migration or is it part of a ceremony the Pope has something to do with?

I was walking to work early one day on the outskirts of the French Quarter near an elementary school, and this pretty black lady, about 35, dressed fit to kill, was standing by the bus stop. Right then a little black dude, no mor'n ten, snatched her purse and started runnin' for the ghetto. You have to understand all this took place in less than a minute. The lady kicked off her high heels and started chasing the kid with her purse, but her speed was no match for him. I started to run after him also. But I was too far behind to be of help. They ran past the elementary school when the lady yelled, "He's got ma purse, he's got ma purse!" A middle-aged fourth grade teacher saw everything and ran out of his classroom, with the whole fourth grade class in pursuit. So this is the deal. The pretty black lady was out of breath. Close behind the purse-snatcher were a teacher and maybe twenty students all runnin' after him. The little delinquent thought he'd lose them by runnin' inside the Iberville Housing Projects in the ghetto. No good.

The teacher and his students ran inside, grabbed

him, and hustled him back to school from which he was playing hooky, this being coincidentally his regular teacher, Mr. Stubbs. The victim, a black lady who said she was on her way to a weekly get-together to play bridge, offered Mr. Stubbs ten dollars for his troubles, but he said no he couldn't take it. In class he presented her the purse like a medal. The whole fourth grade applauded and cheered. I've never seen so many smiles, except maybe at a wedding.

Now it was time to deal with Hershel, Mr. Stubbs' delinquent student. The teacher wore a coat and tie. He was a Creole of color who had studied philosophy at Xavier University where he earned a Bachelor's degree. But he also had credentials as an elementary education major.

Mr. Stubbs placed a desk at the head of the class, told Hershel to take this seat, and began using the Socratic technique on Hershel whom he believed was old enough to listen to reason. It's as if Hershel were in court.

"Hershel," he said, "in eighteenth century Europe, during the Enlightenment, there was a brilliant thinker named Immanuel Kant. He thought a lot about ethics which concerns the way all of us have to live peaceably in society. He came up with an idea he called the Categorical Imperative, which was a kind of universalization test. But I don't expect you to remember that part. What I want you to remember is why stealing is wrong."

Hershel, sitting in the desk facing Mr. Stubbs, hung his head down, ashamed, probably, over what he did.

"Do you know what you did was wrong?"

"Yes, Mr. Stubbs."

"Well, Kant said if we wish to do something, then that wish should be applied to everyone else. And if a person should steal, it follows that everyone else ought to be able to steal. But there is a contradiction here. The question is 'What would happen if everybody in the world kept stealing things?'" "Could you trust anybody, Hershel?"

"No."

"That's right. And is it important for people to trust each other?"

"I guess so."

"Did you ever not trust anybody?

"Yeah."

"How did you feel?"

"I was afraid of him."

"Ah ha, and when you're afraid of someone, is that a good or a bad feeling?"

"It's a bad feeling."

"That's right. In fact, if you're afraid of people you might run away from them, or you might even hurt them by, say, hitting them."

"Yes, Mr. Stubbs, I understand."

"Well, Hershel, I know I wouldn't want to live in a society in which everyone feared everyone else. Would you?"

"No, sir."

"So you see how stealing a purse is a very wrong thing to do?"

"Yes, sir."

I had been standing by the classroom door, listening to this little inquiry. In my heart I thanked Mr. Stubbs for his wisdom and quickly left the doorway.

4.

Soileau, your trouble is you have been cursed by

wanting things which are too much for one man alone.

But bless my father. This is the speech he didn't give. He didn't sit us down at the kitchen table and say: "So here we are on what would have been your mother's and my thirty-fifth wedding anniversary. One son is still living here, having taken no initiative to get out on his own. The second son takes out loans for things he is always falling behind on in his payments. He can't pay for his car, he can't pay to have his teeth fixed, nothin'. I have to pay. Here a daughter doing poorly in school. A sad bunch of birds. And here I am, alone, at the same job for twenty-five years, getting raises each year, making a modest living, owning a home, some land, a car, a toothbrush, milk in the refrigerator for my cereal, some chicken noodle soup in a can with very little chicken, no whiskey, no women. Yes, well, I wouldn't mind my bearing the weight so much, but how you all have betrayed me, all of you with such promising futures. I am unbearably pitiful at times. Do you laugh at me when I sleep?" He never said any of it, but he could have. Oh, the nest is still full of fledglings beginning to gray at the feathers.

And no one told me this either: "The big men, the men at the top ask: how can we keep the cooks from eating the dinners meant for the customers, the bartender from drinking *our* whiskey, the stock boys from taking out a carton of cigarettes under their heavy coats in winter? We can't watch everybody all the time. Everything and nothing haunts us."

Case in point: the black dudes at the restaurant and bar be runnin' aroun' when the manager not lookin', and be askin' me to give them free mixed drinks or beer on the sly. Now I have to tell these guys, I bein' honest Kent, "say listen man, you dudes know I'll lose mah job if de boss man finds out I been givin' you liquor."

Dey be lookin' at me wit a frown. "Bartender," day say sassy, "bartender, you be a hard, hard man."

"Look guys," I say, "ya make me feel bad. I tell ya what. Nex week when I git paid, I'll buy you a drink personally." Pause. "*After* work."

"You gots a deal, bartender," dey say.

Den Sidney ask me fo a dolla. "Damn it, Sidney, I ain't got no dolla! Get lost." Sidney hangs around a while, while I start wipin' de bar. He mopes away. Dat, as dey say, is dat. See Sidney? Spends all his money on pay day. He eighteen. Be stayin' wit his momma. Wants to be a boxer. Always walkin aroun throwin' punches in de air.

And the maître d'? Someday I'monna tell ya somethin' about that bad-assed, nicely-dressed-in-the-finest-tuxedo black dude who used to be de star basketball player on his high school team. Yes, suh. And he'll tell ya he wuz a star. He be sweet on all de waitresses. He call all de cute little waitresses "Baby" the way I do.

No, but I'm real sad today. Willie, the shortest and blackest of all the black dudes, and the best oyster shucker in town, walked in two hours late with his head down. "Hey, Willie," I said, "you look down in the dumps."

"I am, Kent, I am."

He walks to the back, and next thing you know he's stompin' up front, tears off his white oyster shucker's top, says, "Shit, I don't need this damn job," and walks out the front door, slamming it. I run out and yell, "hey, Willie, I want to talk to you." But he disappears into the heavy crowd on Bourbon Street, and I've never seen him again. I am sad because Willie used to tell me everything, how his brother-in-law would always ask him to lend him ten dollars, how he stepped on a snake while walking late at night on the levee of the Mississippi and almost got bit, how his wife threw a butcher knife at him one night. Willie, wherever you are, I wish you'd have talked to me about why you got mad at the boss and quit. Willie, when will you ever learn who your friends are? It's sad, sad.

(I'm writing this on the top of my car in a dim street light on Iberville Street.)

That night I got off work at Li'l Momma's at midnight. Spent twenty minutes, in addition to my usual clean-up duties, cleaning up after some dummy dropped a whole case of Collins glasses. The broken glass in a restaurant is not funny. Most often you'll be in the front, tending bar, and you'll hear the glass crashing in the back near the kitchen. And you think, oh shit.

I remembered leaving my car parked on Dauphine. I walked down Bourbon Street to Conti and took a left. The street cleaners had begun to sweep the streets. June, and two German girls, world travelers, told me at the bar this town had some of the most humid weather they'd ever been in. While they told me this at 5 PM, a police tow truck was towing away the maître d's car which was parked in front of Li'l Momma's in a no parking zone. Brand new American car with Texas license plates. The maître d' was trying to talk the tow truck policeman out of towing his car away, but he couldn't, even though they were soul brothers, so the maître d', a one time basketball great, not only in high school and college, but also professionally, left work early to go to the auto pound and pay fifty dollars to get his car back. Someone had to lend him the money.

Anyway, I walked to Dauphine where I thought my car was. It wasn't there! I felt electric sparks in my belly. For a moment I couldn't remember where I parked it. All the streets looked the same. Narrow streets. Had it been stolen? Then I remembered Iberville Street, the six hundred block by an oyster bar. I pursed my lips in a kind of whistle position and just breathed out.

When I got to my car there was a black dude standing in the middle of two white dudes dressed in green striped bath towel short-sleeve shirts and blue jeans. Off to the left was a uniformed policeman, his hand on his gun in its holster. What the hell? I stood back a ways from them all.

One of the guys in blue jeans told this black dude: "Hey, man, why did you try to sell this man some grass?"

Black dude: "Hey, man, like I dunno nothin' bout no grass." Then it hit me. I had seen something like this in the movie, the *French Connection*, where Gene Hackman played that bad-assed plain clothes man, Popeye Doyle. This must have been a drug bust, too, only on a smaller scale.

"OK, man," the plain clothes cop told the dude, "spread your legs and put your hands on the car." The dude was co-operative. I walked over to the plain clothes man and said, "Excuse me, but this is my car you're using, and I really have to get home." He said: "Police business, son, you'll just have to wait." I wasn't going to argue with anybody with that uniformed policeman there, his hand on his gun.

"Say, man, you gotta knife?

"No, man," said the black dude, his legs spread and his arms stretched, his palms face down on the hood of my VW.

The plain clothes man reached deftly at the black dude's ankles and pulled out a long switchblade.

"No knife, huh?" He handcuffed him, and they all took him away in an unmarked police car.

And oh, I found out what happened to Willie from

a reliable source. The boss told Willie to take off his gold pierced earrings. Willie said: "I don't take off my earrings for nobody." The boss said: "Pick up your paycheck tomorrow. It'll be your *last* one, buddy."

Finally, headed home that night on the Interstate. All the windows in my VW open. The car filled with wind. Fifty-five, sixty, sixty-five.

> *I would like to stop a trucker,*
> *unlike a cop,*
> *and shake his hand,*
> *and tell him what a good job*
> *he's done. "Trucker,*
> *I forgive you."*
> *"Wise man, who has earned your well-being,"*
> *he would tell me, "I forgive you too."*

5.

True, I have forgotten about Mary Lamont, my first real love, for the most part. But there is one bit of irony I'll never forget. One night during the summer I visited her in Savannah. She had just finished her freshman year at Newcomb College in New Orleans. It was July 4th, and that night we had a barbecue at her parents' mansion, built ante-bellum style, with sixteen rooms. She'd invited fifty or more of her friends from Savannah. Her invitation read: "Bring friends and occult libations." It was 9 PM. We were all sitting in the enormous backyard eating rib-eye steaks and potato salad in paper plates. The full moon shone brighter than the candles all around. Someone blew all the candles out. Only the moon. Then Mary's dog, Billy, jumped up to her arm, and began thrusting his lower body with its pink carrot against her. I sensed everyone's embarrassment and called Billy over to me. His excitement quieted as I petted him. I knew Mary was a virgin. Perhaps Billy was trying to tell her something: that the young must come of age, but exactly when, who can say? She was 18 then, I, 21. I have never ever entered her body.

Right now, I have not felt this way in years, in fact since my Mary Lamont episode nine years ago. Perhaps, inside, I have been a bear asleep for nine winters and all the seasons in-between. How, at 30, could I feel jealous of a young waitress I haven't even kissed, when two tall guys walk in the restaurant to talk to her?

Vickie was twenty-one, a senior studying communications at Cornell, and came to New Orleans from Binghamton to get a summer job. She was cute, very soft-spoken, and the strange thing, well, she was six feet three inches tall. Every time we worked the same nights and passed each other during our running around in the restaurant, we would make some kind of bodily contact: a pat on the back, an overdone handshake which made us both laugh, or I would touch a lock of her curly blond hair and tell her what a tremendous head of hair she had.

She had two jobs. Apparently these guys knew her from her other job. They came in, asked for her, and another waitress went to the back to get her. Look it, these guys were no competition for average-height me, even though they were younger, thinner, closer to her age, and as tall as she was.

All three began to talk to each other immediately, a ways away from me. I felt a pain in my stomach. Then I said: "Hey, Vickie, did you know two interesting recent findings? Well, one is that most people who don't like animals don't usually like other people. And if a man doesn't marry before he's thirty he probably never will get married." Vickie sort of smiled. Her two friends looked uncomfortable.

"Oh, Kent, I'm sorry. I want you to meet my two friends, Mitch and Jerry." I reached over the bar, shook their hands, and said nice to meet ya. They both had shoulder length hair. My hair was pretty long too. My eyes made contact with all six of their eyes as I said: "Gee, I sure hope long hair on guys is here to stay. I don't think I'd like the way I'd look with any other shorter hair style."

Mitch looked bored.

But Jerry said: "Yeah, Kent, that's right. I feel the same way."

Jerry: "How's your little finger, Vickie?"

She had cut her little finger opening a can at her other job in a hotel. It took four stitches.

"Oh, it's OK. See, I'm still wearing the bandage, but it gets in my way. The doctor said I shouldn't get it wet, but practically everything I do as a waitress means I have to get it wet. I guess I'm a helpless cripple."

We all laughed. Then I took Vickie's wounded little finger in my hand and kissed it. "There," I said, "you sweetie, that kiss will make it better, oooh, ooh." She laughed, but the two guys didn't. If only I could say enough funny and entertaining things, maybe these guys wouldn't impress her. Jerry talked more than Mitch. Mitch looked like he was just along for the ride, not interested in anything.

Vickie put her hand over the corner of her mouth. "See that guy over there in the last booth? Don't all look at the same time! He was in here with another girl last night, and still another one the night before. See me, I can't stand that type of guy. To top it off he has a British accent."

I had to speak up. "What's the matter, Vickie, can't a man put his money in three banks if he wants to? Who's to say if he got what he wanted from the other two girls?"

"Oh, he probably did. I just know his wine-em-and-dine-em type."

"How were your tips tonight?" Jerry asked her.

"Pretty bad."

I thought I'd add a bit of information. "Yeah, I've heard the dilemmas of waitresses and waiters. If you're overly nice to most people, it spoils them. They say: oh bring this steak back. It's not well-done enough. Of course, if you're not nice and alert, they won't tip well. But then most of them don't tip well anyway."

I sensed these guys wanted to ask her something, and I felt a need to make up a story. "Hey, you know Vickie, kids can really be funny. I called up this divorced woman friend of mine and her nine-year-old girl answered. Is Betsy there? I asked. No, she said, who's this? Me: This is Kent. Are you a friend of my mommie's? "Yes." "A good friend?" "Yes." "How long have you known her?" "Oh, I don't remember." (I heard her call her mother to the phone.) "Are you going to marry my mommie?" (My heart fluttered.) "Uh, well, I don't plan to, at least not right away." Kids sure are somethin', huh Vickie?"

She smiled. "Yeah, really."

"Your kids'll one day probably be lookin' at your little finger and ask you where you got that small scar."

A new waitress came up and asked me to make three drinks. I'm pretty fast at this. I made her a Harvey Wallbanger, a Sloe Comfortable Screw, and a Pina Colada, all in about two minutes. Waitresses and waiters mostly come and go here. Like Willie, quit or get fired, one. The manager's a pretty demanding guy: the type that walks around and asks you abruptly *whatcha doin'*, as if you were doing something you weren't supposed to. I have seen it: how male managers will not be fair with men, and yield to women, and vice versa with female managers. And I have seen myself, and who I am. I am the German teacher who re-taught me how to laugh in 1972. I wear my father's body whose walk I learned, whose hands and gentle voice I use to speak. I am my mother who taught me how to get depressed and think men were tyrants to women, and I am all the men and women, children and animals I ever imitated, forgot, and imitated again. I am a pebble in the tide on the beach, being washed as near to home as the shore is.

There were two guys and a girl, thirtyish, dressed in evening wear, seated at the first booth. They were drinking a lot of wine. No food. The girl was going from one man to the other, kissing and hugging them while they were arguing about problems at the office. They were rude, loud, and every other word was "shit" and "fuck." I walked calmly over to their table.

"Excuse me, but there are other customers here who can hear you clear across the restaurant. Would you please watch your language, and keep your voices lower? Thank you." One man was so drunk he hung his head down. "OK, bartender."

Vickie saw a family with two small babies and went up to the babies to tickle their chins. "Boy, you sure are cute," she said to the babies. The parents were all smiles.

But how many have thought: we sure do have ugly children. I thought: babies make faces at us and how we all like to make faces back at them. But they won't remember us.

They are here and not here. It's as if they were dreaming themselves through life.

Jerry had Vickie giggling about something. Boy, I sure wish I could make girls laugh for more than a minute like that Jerry.

Vickie said she had to go wait on a customer.

"Say Vickie," Jerry said. "We're going floating down the Tangipahoa on inner tubes this Saturday. Wanna come along? Hey, doll, we're really gonna have some fun."

Now, Vickie had once told me this. That she had a big scar on her left leg from a motorcycle accident, and she was self-conscious about wearing shorts or a bathing suit. Her whole family was self-conscious. Her brother grew a pot belly in one year in New York and wouldn't put on a bathing suit to go swimming.

But now. "Oh," Vickie sighed. "Saturday's my day off. I really wanna catch up on my rest. But thanks."

Boy, I felt good. I can't tell you how good I felt. They didn't score.

Vickie left at the end of the summer to go back to New York to start her last year at Cornell in Communications. The only time I kissed her was at the airport. I was so sad I smoked some *Cannabis sativa* (my Bourbon street dealer assured me it was the real thing), and I hallucinated, God knows why, and wrote this:

Henry Ford was skinny and believed everyone should have been skinny. He did not like fat people and fired many. He would have fired me for my fatness. Once Henry Ford gave his production manager a new car for outstanding achievement. "Look, Mr. Ford," he said, "I spend lots of time polishing the wonderful car you gave me." Mr. Ford then fired him because he polished too much and worked his job too little. Henry Ford would have built his home on Mount Everest just to keep his child from being kidnapped. He would have built tanks for Germany in those grim years if they promised to keep the peace. Ford believed strongly in peace. I do, too, but if he invited me over to his house, he would have said, like my Uncle Buster, "You have to take a shower before you sleep in my bed. I don't want to get the sheets dirty."

To which I reply: "I refuse to take a shower. I took one last night, and that's enough. Goodbye, Uncle Buster, Goodbye, Mr. Ford. I am thirty years old and no longer want to be your house guest." Oh, Uncle Henry Ford, Uncle Buster, for the bones there is only the dark night of the body.

And so, anyway, I got fired from Li'l Momma's. Someone was stealing money from the cash register. The management made everyone take a lie detector test. I refused, not because I stole the money — I didn't — but because when I talk I tend to make up too many stories. It's simple. Whoever won't take the test can pick up their pay check and leave.

The other reason I refused was I distrusted the Fascism of it all. A few of my close friends were in tears when I left. I would make 'em laugh so much, my friends couldn't help but want me around. The manager told me I could pick up my check first thing in the morning.

✳

The last time I saw Mr. Raindrinker it suddenly occurred to me that he was wearing the same suit he had worn two weeks before. And it was a tweed winter suit, not at all appropriate for the hot summer weather that was coming to New Orleans.

I stopped by the Rusty Nail bar, and there he was drinking alone in that same suit he was wearing two weeks before.

"Say, buddy, you smell awful. When was the last time you took a shower and changed clothes?"

"I dunno," he said and sipped his beer. "I really don't care."

"Hey, look, remember when you fought as an amateur? And you asked me to feel how tough your biceps was, and you told me to hit you in the chest a coupla times? You were in great shape not long ago."

He was silent.

"Hey, man, what's going on?"

He was still silent. He took a pen from his top pocket and wrote me a note on a napkin:

"Soileau, please come over to my place and help me change. I can't bear to look at my body, if I have to change myself."

Then he put his arm around my shoulder and huddled me close. God he stank. From his coat pocket he pulled out a revolver. In the dark below the bar I couldn't make out the type, though I guessed it was a .38 caliber. Never in my whole life have I ever liked guns so I pushed the thing away from him. He put it back in his coat pocket. Then he wrote me another note on a napkin: "I bought this gun to prove to my ex-wife that even though I had a gun, I wouldn't use it to hurt her."

I said: "God, you've lost a lot of weight. When was the

last time you ate?"

Another note on a napkin: "I dunno. Soileau, I see words before my eyes. I think I can perform miracles. I think—" Silence. I kept asking him questions, but he said nothing, absolutely nothing, and only once did he even look at me. A few times he was about to speak, his mouth opened, but he had nothing to say. It was as if someone switched off the light bulb that was his brain. I became frightened. This was not the same man I knew who was life itself, however sometimes unusual. I led him out of the bar as best I could. He was still heavy even though he had lost a lot of weight. I laid him across the back seat of my car like a piece of lumber.

There was a restaurant next door, if front of which my car was parked. They were putting all the evening's garbage next to the street. Flies swarmed about. Some flew into the back seat. "Be careful, R. D., they're hungry," and I don't know why I said that. "You think they'll eat me?" he said and cried for a few minutes. He picked up the flashlight on the floor of the car, turned it on, and stared into it until I realized he wouldn't quit. So I took it away from him.

He took out a napkin from his coat pocket, clicked his ball-point pen, writing: "My mouth is on crooked, my mouth is on crooked. I have powers. The words I see in front of my eyes are holy. I am Jesus."

I took him to the emergency room of the Hospital of New Orleans. He looked at me: "Hey, Soileau, why did you take me to the police station? I'm no criminal." I looked around and saw only one security guard nearby.

On the third floor, where the mental cases were locked up, the one doctor questioned me about my friend. I told him what I knew. Then he brought Raindrinker into a room where the two of them had the closed room to themselves. I waited in the lobby.

I don't know what happened to Raindrinker, except in my having seen his bizarre behavior when they invited me over for supper. Six weeks ago he seemed OK. I remember his telling me something funny. He said: "You know, Soileau, I swear I have four friends named Dick Tracy, Matt Dillon, James Bond, and Charlie Chan. Every time Matt, Dick, James, and Charlie introduced themselves, their new acquaintances would say, 'Oh, come on, you're kidding,' or: 'Hey, really, you're putting me on.'"

When the two of them emerged from the room, the doctor gave R. D. to two male nurses who led him into a door that was unlocked first, then locked again from the inside.

Now the doctor, fat as a cab driver, played me part of a tape recording of his interview with Raindrinker.

Doctor: How are you feeling now? Any thoughts?

R. D.: I like dead people. You see I don't know. I'm Jesus. (laughs and giggles) Yellow, yellow business espionage-rickety-hippie-astroidization. All these TV people want to think us white folks won't play wagon with them and r-monkey with them.

Doctor: What do you mean by r-monkey?

R. D.: Well, a monkey is an ape, right? And r-monkey is r-ape.

Doctor: I see, I see. Does this mean anything to you: when the cat's away, the mice will play?

R. D.: cats mice lip drain me Jesus alright oh oh oh a million-billion. (Giggles again.)

The doctor asked me if he had any family. I told him his estranged wife was really the only one he had, but at the moment she was determined to see as little of him as possible.

"I see. Well, we'll commit him here for the short term. But we may have to have him transferred to the State Hospital at Grand Chene."

Ah, I knew it well. I thanked the doctor and quickly disappeared.

I'm writing this from far away. It is the end of summer here. The trees are brightly colored. I've never seen my friend since I placed him into the hands of those who could know him better than I could. When I freed him from myself I felt *that* part of my mind securely in the unconscious. I could only dream him now.

Chapter Nine

⚜

1.

I'm not sorry I left Li'l Momma's. Just to show you, every time someone would walk in off Bourbon Street to use the bathroom, we'd have to tell them (manager's orders): "Sorry, folks, our rest rooms are reserved for our customers." What? Sure, I'd be angry, too. Sometimes, when the managers weren't around, I'd let a street walker use the john anyway.

The thought of Li'l Momma's still haunts me. I just know I'll start remembering the place and have to tell. I remember looking out of my window on Bourbon Street, so big it could have been a giant TV screen, and thinking I recognized a high school friend. I thought: Donald Arceneaux. Wasn't he killed in Vietnam? This hulk of a figure who just *had* to play football walked closer. No, it wasn't Donald Arceneaux, whose father coached the high school team, yet I was in the state of seeing him in strange places.

Then there was the maître d', the soul brother all the women were after, whose mere presence made his financial credit good with any woman, who stood at the entrance of Li'l Momma's barking out: Oysters on the half shell. Ten cents apiece. We call it the Lover's Special. One thin dime. The best buy on B. street. Only a few more minutes, folks, then it's all over with.

And all the others I cannot escape, the entertainers and the entertained: the lady from a religion I don't know selling roses and twirling them like a baton to show off; the shoe shine black boy who got four dollars for a one dollar shine; the black ten-year-old, tap dancing in the street, who picks up his box empty of coins and moves on; Missionary Annie in her nun-like white habits, preaching to everyone, anyone, collecting for charity, the heavy silver cross of Christ hanging squarely between her breasts; the hot dog man whose oven is in the shape of a giant hot dog; the amputee in his wheelchair talking all night to the hot dog man; the stripper who left her husband, telling me proudly, "the only man who laid his hands on me and got away in one piece was my daddy, honey"; the cop tugging at the arms of a groggy loser, asleep on a doorstep, wishing his life would go away; and two drunks, each with a big ego, laughing at the teetotalers of Alcoholics Anonymous who are in town for their annual convention, eating a lot to make up for what they can't drink that is all around them.

Two educated drunks talking past each other:

"I got this shirt I'm wearing from the Goodwill. It only cost me a dollar. And you'd pay ten dollars for a decent shirt like this in any department store."

"Right pal. When my door is open at night, the sounds of the soft rain become the sounds of footsteps in another part of the room."

"But seriously, literature is an alternative to the news."

"You're all wrong pal. Can you imagine a bartender

who doesn't smoke?"

"Right, and of course the irony of the French Quarter is that it is all one way streets, but the people aren't all one-way, if you know what I mean."

"So what? So they're out of whipped cream for Irish coffee. You never did like the goddamn stuff anyway."

"Hey, looka this guy with his fat-assed broad. God, anybody who wears wire-rim glasses — I don't know what to think of them. It disgusts me."

"Shit, the world can't be all bad. Every day two people bump into each other by the millions and both of them say *I'm sorry, excuse me.* "

"Jesus Christ, bless Shakespeare, bless Dante, bless Goethe, I suddenly understand what they all mean, only I can't put it in words."

"Yeah, you know sometimes I think if I take off all that covers my feet the wind will get trapped between my toes."

"You know what I think? Somehow a lot of education has a way of placing people out of a world that has to be written about, the world of the weak and the wrong."

"Hey, what'd you say, I was looking at Miss Big Tits here."

"You remember when you were eighteen and never laughed, and took everything so goddamn seriously your peers said: Oh, here comes MR. MATURE."

"Last night, buddy, I gave my dog his food. I was eating ice cream. Never eat with a dog. He cannot make good dinner conversation; which means his food is more important to him than you are."

"Did I ever tell you my parents hate my eighteen-year-old sister's boyfriend because he's a cop and divorced and thirty-four with five kids?"

"Say man, how do I know? I like the short, dumpy, married ones. Say, pal, where did you disappear to?"

And so on. It's sad, sad.

And I am haunted by Mr. Raindrinker. I dream him. He is an angel. "In the car-shell of the human body," I tell him, "there is at least one driver. But the car-shell of the human body may be packed with many more. The more people in the shell, the more discomfort there is for everyone."

He replies: "The human body is more like a space capsule. In 1969, one of the astronauts thought: the moon must be waiting for us. Why else would it have stayed there?" Mr. Raindrinker is an angel.

Tonight I sleep just till the dogs wake up the neighborhood.

I musta lost ten pounds in the past week or so. When it gets this hot, I don't feel like eating much. Also: as a habit of mine lots of diet drinks which now, like smoking cigarettes, are supposed to cause cancer when the saccharine is fed to laboratory animals. How can you win? Once, in high school, my science fair project called for me to use leopard frogs, *Rana pipiens*. My animals kept dying because they couldn't take captivity in an unnatural environment. They won't eat. Only years later, as one who took care of frogs for a biology professor, did I learn you have to pry their mouths open and stuff their small gullets with frozen horse meat to keep them alive. Not knowing this in high school, I tried to tempt them once to eat on their own with live larval worms that wiggled. No good. They would rather die no matter how tempting the food. Bless frogs for their patience. Not guilty! I'd say if they ever were taken to court. They just sit there, their huge eyes not even moving, their souls at the edge of all of our losses.

It was the same thing when I was captive in the State Hospital. The sight of food disgusted me. I would take two bites of mashed potatoes and push my plate away. God, was I skinny then. When my ex-girlfriend came to visit me, she hardly recognized me. I was shrinking in like my tiny Cajun grandfather in the last years of his life.

In some brief moment in the first week of June it occurred to me I would never be a physician. For the first time in my life I had passed up an exit on the Interstate and could not back up because the current was too strong against me. Forget it, Soileau. All your life the Renaissance man was only barely out of reach. It's over now. Relax. No other man in no other place, but now. Prufrock realized who he was not, so can you. Know this: to make love is not to have an orgasm every time. It's just the simple, gentle rhythms, it's playing opposite to your grandfather cutting trees with a cross-cut saw, easy back and forth, it's playing the violin not so much to finish the song as to make a music of the mind.

2.

When my father told me the news tonight of my great-uncle's impending death at 68, two hundred miles away from my life, I was not really shocked, just a little sad, because I had not seen him or any of my other dozens of Cajun relatives on my father's side in fifteen years.

For several years, beginning coincidentally on my twelfth birthday, Uncle Zanon drove the rural route for Seaport Coffee Company out of Beaumont, Texas. All the southwest Louisiana country folks drank coffee in those days — and maybe even since the Cajuns came in the middle of the eighteenth century — so it was a way for Uncle Zanon to make a living. (He just didn't have the luck to be a rice farmer, many of whom got rich.)

On Sundays my Tante Bernice would get to thinking, and say, cooking rice and gravy and meat: "Zanon, mais you in dat truck, drivin' all day long, Monday through Saturday. You know, you jus might get in a bad wreck. Zanon? Mais listen Zanon, Écoute-moi!"

But when she turned to the kitchen sink to wash the dishes scraped clean of rice and meat and gravy, he'd sneak away and go to the front porch to get some fresh breeze in summer under the live oaks, and from my spot, playing marbles alone in the dust, I'd hear him whistling. And all the while he'd be leaning back on the rear two legs of a wooden chair, one covered with an animal's hide, and picking his teeth with a toothpick and spitting out the little pieces of pork from a tasty Sunday roast.

Today, in the darkest corners of a closet that smells of old clothes, I found an old Texaco map of Louisiana my father had given me long ago. I went to the throne and sat there looking at this map. My finger traced the towns Uncle Zanon and I drove through, on Saturdays, in the summer of 1960, from Basile, Louisiana to Beaumont, Texas. We would get up in the darkness of 4 AM, dress, eat quickly, and drive all morning to Beaumont to pick up the coffee and spices he would deliver the following week to fifty small grocery stores in Evangeline Parish. We would get back late from Beaumont, in the dark life of crickets.

My fingers follow the line on the map and I repeat to myself the names of the towns: Elton, Kinder, Ragley, DeQuincy, Starks, and after that the long, townless drive, into Beaumont itself.

For a constipated child of twelve the best cure is to ride two hundred miles round-trip in a truck that vibrates. "It'll shake the shit out of anybody," Uncle Zanon tells me and winks.

I remember wanting to shift gears when we started. "I wanna shift."

"Ok, mon petit," he said, pressing in the clutch. "Do first gear, no, no, first gear," and the gears would make a terrible noise as the engine raced and roared for an instant, then died back down.

"I'm sorry, mon oncle, I did it wrong."

"Mais, ça c'est bon, mon petit. Try again."

"When can I drive by myself, Uncle Zanon?"

"Mais cher, when you get big."

And then silence, the sultry wind blowing hard through my wide open window, passing Elton, and into Kinder.

My favorite hideout was in the back of this truck, me, an Indian with a cap gun, breathing in the smell of fresh coffee, dark roast, medium roast, light roast; and all the spices — ginger, nutmeg, anise — until my whole mind was swirling with spices and I fell asleep, dreaming I had given away all the contents of the back of his huge truck to the Indians.

Those are my only memories of him, that every Saturday morning, early, and in my twelfth summer, he would waken me in the darkness with a cup of coffee in his hands, and let me sip, till I was alive again.

3.

I had not been to the Rusty Nail to hear live music in months. The Cajun band was still playing on Thursday nights. When I got there, the accordion player and band leader Alphonse, whose parents were Cajuns from Opelousas, Louisiana, shook my hand. I explained to him why I had not been there in so long—I worked at Li'l Momma's every Thursday night. He shrugged his shoulders. Then he said partly in French:

"Eh bien, mais it's good to see you, cher."

I kissed his girlfriend on the cheek. She was a beautiful girl of twenty with a perfect nose and perfect lips. We remembered each other from months before. After the usual pleasantries I asked her where she went to high school. Turns out she went to Holy Angels, the same as my sister. We all said what a small world it was. Alphonse went up to the bandstand on stage and they started to play perhaps the most famous waltz in the whole Cajun repertoire: "Jolie Blonde." It was wonderful, except the drummer was a tad loud.

"Oh, Jolie Blonde," Alphonse sang, and in my mind I saw myself, a good waltzer on the dance floor, and in my head I was going 1-2-3, 1-2-3, 1-2-3.

I asked Alphonse's girlfriend to dance.

"Oh, no, sorry Kent," she blushed, "I can't waltz."

"Come on," I said, "I'll lead you. Let's try."

"Please, Kent, I can't."

"Ok," I said, "someday I'll have to teach you."

It seemed everybody was dancing. I wanted to get up on the floor badly. I looked across the room, and there was the girl I waltzed with months before, who told me I was a good dancer. She was there! I walked up to her, and when she recognized me, she hugged me. I couldn't think of her name. And, somehow, like a fool, I didn't ask her. She wanted to waltz, too. We laughed and giggled throughout the whole dance as I led her back and forth, side to side over the whole floor. She knew I was good. The audience knew I was good. I knew I was good. I felt great. The music was loud, and I could barely hear her on the dance floor. She whispered in my ear: "I'm going back to my parents in Milwaukee next week."

I was crushed. Here was the girl I had had the most fun with in ages, and she was leaving town, maybe for good. The dance ended, and she hugged me with a smile. "I'll go get a drink," I said, already half-loaded and went to the bar to get another Southern Comfort on the rocks.

Spilling half my drink, meandering through the heavy crowd, I returned to our spot, but she was gone! I looked around. Shit! I thought. If only I'd had the chance, I would have talked her into staying here in New Orleans.

Anyway, Alphonse's band, La Bete Noire, took a break. I walked up to the table where Alphonse and his beautiful girlfriend were sitting. Alphonse started talking to me in Louisiana French as he had done months before when we met and I told him my family was Cajun. I understood everything he said, but it was so long since I'd spoken it, that I could only think in my other language, German. Miraculously the French came back with a little thought.

I said: "Je comprends tout ce que tu me dis, mais il faut que je pratique plus souvent."

"That's good," he said, "come over to visit with me and my parents and we'll practice Cadien."

"OK, Alphonse." And I thought for an instant that I've been an outsider not only to my own culture, but the French-speaking culture of my parents as well.

I left the Rusty Nail wondering if there was any way in the world I could locate the girl I waltzed with, who was leaving for good soon, for Milwaukee, Wisconsin.

It's sad, sad.

I stumbled into the Rusty Nail a week later pretty drunk, well, looking to dance, knowing I had lost track of the girl who left for Milwaukee. Near the door there was this man filling up a machine with packs of cigarettes and emptying the coins into a small cloth sack. If I were an ornithologist, I would have known exactly what bird sounds he was making. It sounded something like a mockingbird. Boy, was he talented. And no one of everyone there except me complimented him for his talent.

The girl with me was a waitress I'd picked up at Li'l Momma's when she got off work at eleven. She was twenty-two and couldn't dance, so I kissed the few girls there I knew who were already spoken for. Then I danced until 2 or 3 AM. All I remember is asking the girl I was with for a kiss. "I thought we were just friends," she said, composed.

"Hell no," I said, non-composed. I don't remember taking her home, or how I got home.

I woke up the next day at four in the afternoon, the air conditioner with its endless hush. No need to set the alarm clock anymore. No job. I thought: I wonder if my father used my car to go to work with? I remember his saying his own engine blew up, and he needed mine to get to work. Was that a dream? It must have been because my father pulled up in the driveway just then, and his car looked fine.

But the Rusty Nail: the chairs were scattered, the pictures on the walls were crooked, and the bottles of liquor were soldiers in formation at attention.

"Dead to the world." That's what my mother would have said to anyone who witnessed me snoring, mouth open, my body all crooked, half the sheet on me, half of it off. And: "It breaks my heart." That's my mother after I upset her. "Every dog has his day. A man can only do so much." Those two by my father.

So my platitudinous father is home. It is my deepest wish to hold a job as long as he has. I'm not kidding now. My deepest wish.

Not two minutes after my father settled in to his rocker to watch the news, and I opened a book of poems, I heard the rat trap snap shut. My father must have heard it, too, cause we met on the breezeway by the washing machine. Not one rat, but two baby rats caught by the iron pincher were flapping around, not yet willing to die. If rats weren't so damn secretive, if they didn't plot against us in their dark corners, perhaps we could be friends. Actually, I have no other deep feelings about rats.

I wanted to talk about the land I live on in East Gentilly, a virgin marshland until a bulldozer leveled it to a pig farm in 1946, a land Andrew Jackson may have set foot on in 1815. Even if we deny our lives, we cannot deny history.

But let this message suffice: In America, sometimes, we have to look at our words twice. They don't always look like they're spelled right the first time. Really.

Catching rats at home gave me an idea. I didn't have the guts to be a salesman because I couldn't believe enough in anything I had to sell. Selling encyclopedias had been awful. In fact, when salesmen come to my door, I am not rude verbally, I just lower my eyes, not to make initial contact, and gently close the door. I believe in preparing for some ethical speech a politician gives, but I take no stock whatsoever in buying the crap they fill salesmen's minds with these days.

So now I narrowed all my job possibilities to being a

human scarecrow. I take care of unusual kinds of pests. I ran an ad in the paper last week and so far I've gotten three replies. The ad said: I'll get rid of anything you got but don't want. Call the human scarecrow at 381-0001.

Last Monday night I got a hate call from someone threatening to file a class action suit against me for my reducing the pigeon population. This man also said if I didn't stop my pigeon-pogrom on Tuesdays and Thursdays at the Simpson Shipbuilding Yards on the Mississippi, he would shoot flat the tires of my car. I quickly had my phone number changed to an unlisted number, and told my father not to say "Soileau residence" anymore every time he answered the phone.

It was no big deal, actually. My distant uncle, a German chemist, invented a kind of very sticky glue, which, if a pigeon landed on it, would keep it from flying away. He'd be stuck forever.

If I put the glue around the shipyard on Tuesday morning, by nightfall I would have glued down so many pigeons you could hear the sound of wings flapping desperately for miles around. I thought it was being humane. Instead of letting them flap themselves to death, I would go up to each one personally, like a priest giving communion, and gently tap the thing dead with a stick.

Yesterday, Monday the 25th, I got a letter from some big-shot lawyer saying the case was before a judge, and he soon expected a ruling that I could not "glue pigeons to death." He suggested I shoot them, naturally, and with a sportsman's sense of honor, he said shooting at them would at least give them a chance to fly away. The lawyer, it turned out, was the president of some duck-hunting club.

Anyway, Tuesday morning, taking the lawyer's

advice, (for this shipyard was paying me to kill, however I chose to kill) I brought my deceased grandfather's 20-guage shotgun to the #2 Dock on the Mississippi River and opened fire, of course in the direction of the river, away at least from people. I did pretty well actually. I fired just one shot which only managed to scare hundreds of pigeons away. However, I soon heard a siren and saw flashing lights. Later that night my father got me out of jail. I was arrested for disturbing the peace and firing a weapon in a populated area. (I took it to mean populated with pigeons.)

Later in the week a guy named Jones, who raised German shepherds in a yard the size of a public swimming pool, contacted me through a friend to get rid of an infestation of fleas. I sprayed some chemicals of my own mixing and the next day the neighbors on either side of Mr. Jones complained of millions of fleas in *their* yards. It seems the fleas didn't die, but simply relocated where there were no chemicals. Could I get rid of them? the neighbors asked. I realized my incompetence and asked if they could get themselves another boy.

I knew this whole insane way of making a living was becoming scandalous, but I decided to give it one more try.

A farmer, fifty miles away in Tangipahoa Parish, heard of me somehow. He complained of thousands of birds eating his strawberry crop. I decided to intricately time-set explosive devices in the strawberry patches to scare away the birds with noise. In vain. Not only did the explosives blow the strawberries to pieces, but neighbors from the area complained to the Justice of the Peace of possible hearing-loss from excessive noise. With impending legal action on my hands, I decided to hide out in my room for a while (fortunately, I left no one in Tangipahoa Parish with any clues as to my whereabouts) and check the newspapers for some job, any job.

I can say this now, pure and simple: I'm slowly losing some part of me. Do I even like my name anymore? I'm writing this from far away, as I mentioned about the time of Raindrinker's loss to the lock-up for the mentally ill.

I'm somewhere in Texas. Again, the pears under this tree are good. They're the green kind of canning pears, the same kind my grandmother had in her yard for years. The trees are brightly colored and are speaking to themselves in the language of tree. I rode my bicycle here. It took many weeks of camping out on the road, mostly in stranger's barns without their knowing it. I figure I've come four hundred miles. Thank God it's summer. Traveling four hundred miles in deepest winter on a bicycle would have been tough.

As I said in the beginning I thought I would have to hide out somewhere, after the people I revealed in this story would come looking for me in anger. As it turned out, I had to come this far into Texas for quite another reason.

A Tuesday morning in August and my bank calls me. They've stopped payment on another check because they say that's not my signature. They say I can't be the Kent Soileau who wrote the check since the signature doesn't match the one they have on file. That makes three times in three weeks they've done this to me, and each time I've had to go down there to straighten out the mess.

The first time I wrote a check to Phil, the bartender at the Rusty Nail. I was drinking then so I understand how my signature could have looked strange. But the other two times I was stone sober. I wrote one to the drug store and one to the grocery store. Damn, I'm beginning to wonder about myself. First of all I'm left-handed, have always had a poor penmanship (the nuns said that was my character), and it really has been hard for me to write with my hand always covering the words I leave behind. But hell, how could my signature change on me in just three weeks' time?

I had to drive to the bank to straighten out the whole mess once again.

Then it happened. I was stopped in a parking lot about ten or fifteen feet behind this old banged-up Chevy. Suddenly the woman driver throws it in reverse and starts backing into me very, very fast. I blow my horn. Too late. Bang! My whole front end, headlights and all got smashed in. I got out of my car, furious as hell. "Hey, lady, what the hell ya doin'?" She gets out of her car, puts her hand on her neck and starts moaning.

"Oh my neck, my neck." I should have found some witnesses to say what really happened, but the thought didn't occur to me.

I caught a glimpse of a man standing near the car. He wore a plain, dark T-shirt and black jeans. His gaunt frame, his cough, and a few bits of tobacco in his salt-and-pepper question-mark-like head of hair, suggested a lifetime of smoking. Perhaps he even rolled his own cigarettes — using packaged tobacco and cigarette papers you licked — for it would have been cheaper that way. Later, waiting for the cops, I could hardly see him in the gathering darkness, they blended in so well.

The cops finally came three hours later. All that while the lady was moaning and I didn't say anything, knowing it wasn't my fault. In the meantime several people who just stood there and watched appeared where there were none before. I'd offered to console the woman, but she pushed me away. The cops asked both of us what happened. Before I could say anything five or six people came up as witnesses and testified to the two cops that I ran into her from the rear. What the hell? Then the man with the salt-and-pepper question-mark-like head of hair came up from the darkness, yelling at me: "I'll see you in court, man, I'll just see you in court!" I couldn't speak I was so stunned. The cop told me he would file a report that I hit her in the rear since there were witnesses in her behalf. I suddenly felt dizzy in the heat. It must have been a hundred degrees. An ambulance came for the woman who had neck pains. I grew even dizzier, looking at my bashed-in hood and fender. Who was going to pay to have it fixed? I myself had no insurance. All I remember is the cops getting in their cars with their faces showing no emotion whatsoever, and the black man in black jeans shouting again in my face: "She's hurt bad, we'll see you in court, man!"

Friday night. From my window I watch the moon, more orange and as large a coin as I have ever seen. Strange moon. When will spring come and withdraw from me all the sadness of the tiny child within me? Patience, Soileau, patience.

So, for me a movie on TV. The beautiful child I see in the film with Greer Garson should be about forty-five years old now. Where have the years taken him?

For the past week I've been dreaming like crazy. I don't usually remember my dreams. But now, for example:

Dream One. Raindrinker has been haunting me. He was a strange bird, as my father would say. I dream him going to the opera simply because he wanted to clap his hands. But not because he enjoyed the performance. No. You see, he knew clapping for the final bows lasted so long his hands would swell up. Well, he couldn't go around town clapping. People would think him strange. So he clapped even harder than everyone else at the opera. Every Saturday night (at least it seemed so in the dream) he would go home to his wife with his hands pitifully swollen, and she would soak them in hot water, all the while kissing him full on the hands and lips and ears and every exposed part of his body as he undressed.

Dream Two. I'm in court for rubbing myself against the buttocks of a woman whom I approached from the rear. The judge is an ape.

"So," the ape-judge says, "you have only one witness to say you didn't try to enter the plaintiff from the rear. My friend, Mr. Soileau, your witness has such bad eyesight, he has such thick lenses that the court considers him blind for the court's purposes."

"But, your Honor!"

"Enough," he says. "The plaintiff has twenty-five scientists with a microscope on each left eye and a telescope on all the other right eyes to say you tried to enter her from the rear. Also, if necessary, all of these scientists can see in the dark like owls. What have you to say to that?"

"Your Apeness, I'm speechless."

Then the whole situation no longer seemed like a burlesque. I clutched my stomach tightly. Whenever I get upset it hits me in the stomach, like Bill Young, who when we were eight, punched me and knocked the wind out of me. My God, his fist is still deep in my belly.

4.

Dick Cavett, my friend, you whose voice is as gentle as Groucho's, you ask me why things keep recurring in my work? When I yank out nails from an old piece of lumber, I save them, and use them again to build something else.

Dick, give people Interstates and they'll bitch about two-lane highways. Give 'em air-conditioning and they'll whine about the common fan. It spoils them.

A final note about my brother whom I've not seen in ages, but who's coming over now as much as twice a week. The point is he and his wife speak very little to me and my father when they come over to spend the night.

My father whispers in my ear while they are cleaning out the refrigerator of food: "Those two birds just come over to use my washer and dryer, eat my food, watch my TV, and uh, sleep in my beds. I'll have to tell them they better start talkin' to me like human beings should. You think I'm bein' too tough?"

"No, Dad," I say, "you're not bein' too hard on them. If that's the way you feel, tell 'em."

I have spoken.

It was Sunday morning when I heard knocking at my front door. Thinking it was a salesman, or worse even, a beggar, I only cracked the door and peeked out. No one but salesmen, beggars, religious fanatics trying to convert us, or people from the March of Dimes or Heart Association (these latter two I don't mind) ever comes to our front door. As I may have said, my father and I have very few friends.

There is an elderly woman in a uniform. My first thought: what the hell's someone in a uniform doing here on a Sunday? Isn't Sunday supposed to be a day when official-looking people don't work?

"Mr. Soileau?" she asked politely.

"No."

"This is for Kent Soileau."

"What is it?"

"A summons to appear in court."

I had to think fast. I didn't want to go to court and risk losing all I had, which wasn't much, but enough. In the meantime I'd called a black dude friend of mine I once worked with at Li'l Momma's and told him my story about the accident. He told me if you're the car in the rear and the person in front of you lies and says you hit him or her, when it was really the other way around, the court will decide against the car in the rear, no matter what. He's a pretty confident dude, and I'm a pretty good judge of character, so I felt he knew what he was talking about.

"I'm not Kent Soileau. He doesn't live here anymore. I'm his brother."

"Could you tell me where he lives?"

"No, ma'am."

"Did he leave a forwarding address?"

"No, he surely didn't."

She didn't seem annoyed or anything. With nothing else to say, she walked to her car. Then I thought: what if the woman who hit me or the man I assumed to be her husband came around with the police and made a positive identification of me! Lately I've been wanting to leave this place anyway.

I guess I'm as much to blame as the indigent black man is. If I had paid for liability insurance (which is the law), my insurance company would have to settle, and I wouldn't be in the mess I'm in.

One thing I like about my father. He knows exactly when to stop talking. I guess negotiators have to learn that for success in their jobs. Unlike most people these days who ramble, he's not by any means long-winded.

So he found me stuffing things in my old Boy Scout knapsack that I had used many times before to go camping, and I'm talking about fifteen years ago. It still had several lives to it.

"You going some place?"

"Yeah, I'm leaving, Dad. Would you hand me those forks and knives and that mess kit?"

"Why?" he asked.

"I can't explain now. I'll write you a letter when I get where I'm going."

"OK. But remember. You know how sensitive you are about making changes. With a big change in your life, you might just end up with a big zero in the dust."

"I'll be OK."

It's funny how people who know you from years back, but have not kept in touch, will still think of you. A few days ago an old high school friend called the house. I wasn't there. My father said she had read the obituaries in the daily newspaper and saw a "Kent Soileau" had died. She called to make sure it wasn't me. She didn't leave her name. Bless her heart anyway.

I sold my smashed up car to a junk yard, mainly for what the engine's parts were worth, for only about fifty dollars: all I could get I was in such a hurry. It was one of the few things I had besides my books and a few clothes. But my father had some mutual funds in my name worth a hell of a lot of money. I just knew if I got sued the courts would somehow get all that. And who knows if the courts wouldn't try to get something out of my father?

In my knapsack from the Boy Scouts, I had put a sealed envelope with a stamp, one containing a poem I wrote to my father. I couldn't bear to give it to him in person, so I planned to drop it in a mail box as I bicycled out of New Orleans.

The poem went like this:

PORTRAIT

Every morning in the trenches
they told him: synchronize watches.
Now he is watchless.

I've had enough of time, he says,
and turns to me, my father, my older self.
His only other words all day:
Where have my azaleas gone?
What happens to men when they fail to talk?
How many silences must a man have
to tell him he is spring
and not winter in the blood?

He could be thinking of drifting
on a raft out into sea,
of how beautiful to have

golden hair, or dark hair, or no hair
like he has, except for wisps
around the temples.

As much as he is of me,
his life cannot be mine.
If I accept my days
of animals, of sun,
he may not his.
And death? Let him die
in the house of his wife,
children. Let no doctor
attend his bedside.

Already his bones have traveled
all along with his flesh.
Let the earth open his eyes.

I was wearing shorts and a plain white T-shirt with my knapsack on my back and my sleeping bag anchored down. I'm a good cyclist in city traffic. I know how to keep speed with the cars and weave in and out of traffic gracefully. It's amazing how there are no bicycles on the streets, only cars and trucks. I never even had a close call, little and fragile me compared to cars and trucks. I looked for a mailbox at the corner of Tulane and Carrollton on my way west. Then it hit me. Why should I mail my father this insane poem? It's all wrong! All wrong for now! I've got him dying years before he's ready. He would not understand it's a tribute to him early. He might not even understand the poem. That's it. No one can see it until after this earth's had its fill of him. I didn't drop it in the mailbox. No, I would keep this poem in my knapsack, maybe forever.

5.

Now I no longer have to look in my father's kitchen cabinet at all the bottles of medicines my mother had to take before she died. And my medicines. And Dad's. High blood pressure pills. Nerve pills. Arthritis pills. Liver pills. Prednisone. Librax. Valium. Darvon. Tofranil. Dalmane. Maalox. Benadryl. Haldol. Sleeping pills. A damn pharmacy. They slept a sleep of their own, and each had its appointed place. Forget all that.

At the end of September I was at the top of a hill approaching Austin from the south, having bicycled through LaGrange and Bastrop. There was the smell of bread from a bakery nearby. At sunset over the horizon, maybe ten miles out, I could see the State Capitol and the tower of the University of Texas. I felt chills on my neck. I'd heard good words about this place. The locals told me they didn't want any more people: it was growing too fast. So the outskirts of Austin would be where I'd set up camp, small as it would be. I helped a trucker change a flat tire the next mid-morning, and he gave me a beer and some fried chicken. Just for the hell of it I thought I'd bicycle into town and register with the State Employment Service. It was a clinical smelling place, plastic chairs, and you had to wait a long time to see anyone. Finally a man walked up to me and signaled me to his desk with his index finger. I was pretty raggedy looking. I remember his eyes didn't look up to meet mine.

Monotone: "What's your name, please?"

"Soileau."

"What? How ya spell it?"

"My name is Soileau. It's French, pal — if you'd look at me — it's French with an *e-a-u* at the end pronounced like the letter *o*." I said this impatiently. I was thinking of D. H. Lawrence, how he was the spitting image of one of my poet friends, and how I was beginning to learn the silence of stones with all their tiny eyes open. I suddenly felt the need to hold still, to feel, but not to speak.

Perhaps even now I've learned how to live my life. I've changed a lot from all honest and polite Kent, the person that was me a year before my ex-girlfriend had me committed to the State Hospital. It's sad, sad, but I now have little patience in such situations. Never even offered to shake my hand. But so it is with the dull clerks and officials of America who don't know foreign languages. Misspell my name now, but damn it, not on my tombstone.

About Ken Fontenot

KEN FONTENOT received an MA in German Language and Literature from the University of Texas at Austin and studied in Freiburg, Germany under a DAAD fellowship in 1986-87. His second book of poems, *All My Animals and Stars*, won the Austin Book Award, and his poetry collection *In a Kingdom of Birds* won the 2012 Texas Institute of Letters award for best poetry book in Texas. In 2015 a fourth book of poems, *Just a Trace of Moon*, appeared from Pinyon Publishing. His translations of contemporary Geman poems have appeared widely. A New Orleans native, Fontenot lives and works in Austin.

About Mina Zavala Lanzas

Artist *MINA ZAVALA LANZAS* created the artwork used on the cover of *For Mr. Raindrinker*. Born and raised in New Orleans, she is a self- taught artist with training in drama, in music and in languages. Her internationally collected work mixes reality and imagination and is exhibited at Berta's and Mina's Antiquities Gallery on Magazine Street in New Orleans. Lanzas says of her art, "...this is our second line, our dancing through adversity which brings all the cultures together."